A VEGGIE LOVE TALE

Pounded BY PRODUCE

G.M. FAIRY

Content Warning

Dedication

To everyone with religious trauma. I hope this helps heal you in some small, very weird way. Also to Andrew Scott. This is all your fault.

1

Emily

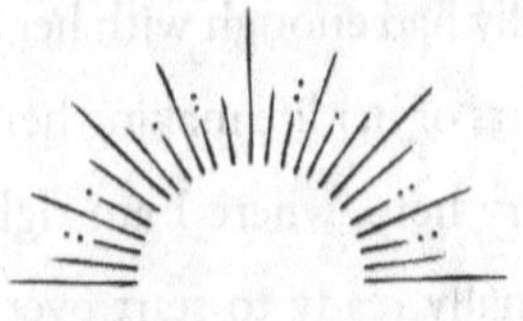

The land of opportunity exists in the crisp corners of a freshly printed newspaper, tucked away in the help wanted section, where every ad promises the world and delivers. At least that's what I tell myself instead of the depressing truth, that it's basically where hope goes to chill in sweatpants and binge-watch bad TV. Who even looks for jobs in a newspaper anymore? Someone who doesn't have internet or reliable transport to the local library, aka me. You don't need recruiter websites when you have the salt of the Earth splayed across your neighbor's driveway. It's not like they'll miss their Sunday paper. They don't even read the newspaper. I mean, I don't think they do.

Between "overnight janitor" and "human sign holder," I can barely contain my excitement about my promising future. It's the scene of every heartwarming rom-com. The mousey brunette sits at her scratched-up bistro table in an oversized t-shirt and underwear she's owned since high school. Her socked feet are tucked under her on the chipped wooden stool as the morning rays shine through her kitchen window, revealing the peeling wallpaper and laminate tile surrounding her. It's the start of a new beginning. Of course, they don't show the messy part where she finally had enough with her deadbeat boyfriend who wasted five years of her life making her feel worthless.

We start the story here, where I am right now. Done with the bullshit and finally ready to start over and make a better life for myself. The problem is that the "opportunities" sitting before me don't give off the shiny new beginning vibes I hoped for. Someone has to do these jobs. I mean, what would we do without our faithful Parking Lot Attendants? But I just wish it didn't have to be me.

Isn't there a place that's looking to hire a socially awkward, clumsy, slow-moving, funny (to herself and like two people) girl who likes to cook and water plants? And while we're here in the land of make-believe, can't it be a place that offers room and board—so I can get out of this shithole mobile home my Uncle Gary's letting me stay in—and enjoy some goddamn peace and quiet? Beggars can't be choosers, but a girl can dream.

I sigh, flipping to the back page, feeling more hopeless than I did when I came home and found the green vase handed down to me by my grandmother, smashed into a million pieces on the floor.

"This is your fault, Emily," he said. "You're the one who forgot to buy the mini sausages for the game tonight. You know how I get when I'm hungry and angry."

I wish I could say that it had been my breaking point, but no, I stayed for another year after that. I guess in the end, most of us end up like our mothers. Except, it's not the end. I got out, and I'm going to make a better life for myself, whether that better is working at a Toll Booth or my dream job.

I fling the paper to the table, deciding it's better to skim through my soulless options with some food on my stomach. The newspaper slides off the table and glides to the floor. I sigh but don't pick it up. Instead, I make my way to the fridge, pulling open the rusted handle and examining its contents. I should know what's in the fridge, but its emptiness shocks me every time.

It wasn't like we were rolling in dough when I was with Darrell. He could never keep a job for longer than a few months, but he always did have a job or the prospect of a new one. I, on the other hand, was never allowed to work. At first, I thought it was endearing; he wanted to take care of me, but then, as time went on and his control slowly reared its ugly head, I realized it wasn't endearing, far from it. I was hopeless, feeling that I had no option but to stay with him because there wasn't a dollar to my name, and a huge gap in employment marked my already unimpressive resume. But then my Uncle Gary told me about this place when he saw me at the grocery store last month. I hadn't been allowed to see my family much, so he already knew something wasn't right, but I think he could tell from the skittish way my eyes darted. He offered me a way out, and I jumped on it, asking him to drive me to Darrell's house so I could collect my few belongings and leave.

My Uncle Gary didn't stop there. He beat the shit out of Darrell once he showed up. Told him if he ever tried to contact me again that he knew plenty of places to hide a body. I'm thankful for my Uncle Gary, I truly am. He's probably one of the only people in the family that's not a piece of shit, myself included. But I can't stay here. He's got his own children to worry about. I need to get a job that allows me to move away from this town. Even if it takes several years, I need distance from the pain of the last five years.

I surrender to my search, grabbing a stale piece of bread, wishing I had produce like onions, tomatoes, cucumbers, something to make an omelet. I don't even have a toaster, so I bite into the starchy morsel as I return to my job-searching post. As I grab the paper, something grabs my attention in the bottom right-hand corner. It's as if a supernatural force pulls all my focus to the tiny black letters amongst a sea of typography.

"Help Wanted: Live-In Parish Cook - Remote, Rural location."

I nearly poop my pants, rubbing my eyes to see if the malnutrition is consuming my eyesight. I reread it a few more times until I finally believe it's real. I sure as shit don't know what a parish is and don't have any way to Google it, but for a remote, rural, live-in cook job, I'd work just about anywhere. My fingers shake as I type in the number on the old landline adhered to the wall. The job seems too good to be true, and I have half a mind to ask whoever picks up the phone whose dick I have to suck to get the position because I most definitely will suck a few penises to get out of this dump and be able to make myself a goddamn omelet.

Thank God, my intrusive, inappropriate thoughts lose because the person on the other line answers. "Thank you for calling St. Mary's Catholic Church. How can I help you?"

2

Robert

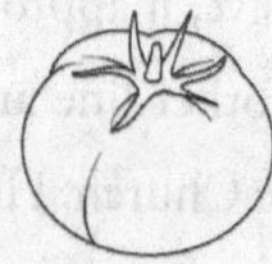

The warm evening sun shatters through the canopy of leaves overhead and splinters into my eye. The irritating rays bring me out of my head and to the realization that several hours have passed. *Fuck*, I think to myself, *I've got a sermon to write.* It's an odd thought—the curse word coupled with the duty to spread God's word, but I can't help it. No matter how hard I pray, I can't scrub the words thrown around my childhood home from my brain. Growing up in a family riddled with poverty, broken marriages, abuse, and crime will do that to a person. Luckily, I'm able to keep my dirty words—and thoughts—to myself, at least most of the time, and never in front of my congregation.

I lean down to pick a ripe and juicy tomato, giving it a tender squeeze before placing it in my basket of other vegetables from the parish garden. It's been three hours since I set out to collect produce for tonight's dinner. I'm a shit cook, but we've had to make do since our cook left two weeks ago. He met a woman and moved to Spain to be with her. For ol' Frances' sake, I hope it's legit, but when it's five p.m., and I'm fucking up spaghetti sauce—I secretly hope he landed in Madrid to find the beautiful young woman he'd been talking to is really a forty-year-old computer nerd with a boil. It's a horrible thought, but the devil gets in my brain when I'm hungry. Thankfully, Gail informed us we will have a new cook tomorrow, hurrah! Maybe then I won't be distracted by the Earth's beauty and finally get my mind on the Lord's word.

"Have you seen my hairbrush?" Laurent yells across the field from the back kitchen door. I whip my attention to him as he rushes toward me, all legs and arms flailing behind his tall form.

I shake my head when he's still several paces away. He sulks, looking up at the clouds and screaming, "Oh, where is my hairbrush!"

I laugh at his dramatics before walking toward him. You'd think after all the years we've known each other, his over-the-top performances due to minor inconveniences would get under my skin, but alas, Laurent never bores me. His constant humor spills from his pores and has a way of melting into the cracks of my hard exterior.

"Robert, oh Robert," he falls against me, out of breath and gripping my shoulder. "Look at me. I'm a mess. He throws the back of his hand over his eyes. What will the patrons think when they see my incurable bedhead?"

I push him off me, and he sputters into a laugh. "I doubt anyone will notice once they hear my sermon."

"Oh, come on, you are a beautiful speaker." He swings his arm over me, kissing the top of my brown curly head. "You can't keep comparing yourself to my divine public speaking skills."

I push him off me, and he stumbles with a laugh. I smile and shake my head. "I know I am a brilliant speaker. I just haven't had time to write a sermon. I've been too busy playing a fucking housewife." Okay, maybe I don't always hide my dirty mouth, at least not with Laurent.

"Oh, don't pull that shit. Have you seen the kitchen? If you were my wife, I'd fire you last week." I'm thankful my partner priest has as much, if not more, of a naughty mouth as I do. Life would be rather drab in this quiet country parish without Laurent to banter with.

I laugh and shove him. He stumbles, grabbing my arm and pulling me to the damp earth. I fall next to him, laughing as I look up at the sky melting into creamsicle hues amongst the puff of white clouds. Our laughs die down, and I settle into the peace of the moment. Birds chirp in the distance. The smell of freshly cut grass wafts around me, and the cool breeze dries the sweat from my brow.

Laurent quiets next to me, and his hand rubs against mine, lazily brushing tender touches against my fingers. I must be so exhausted from being out in the sun and so at peace now that I don't register his intimate touch, instead leaning into it, splaying out my hand for his fingers to dance across my flesh.

My mind wanders as if about to drift off into a dream. Laurent and I have been best friends since seminary school. We've never been afraid to touch each other in a friendly manner—rubbing shoulders, fake sincere kisses on the head, arms intertwined, normal bloke exchanges. I can't deny the zap of electricity that zips through me every time his skin meets mine, but I attribute the sensation to the lack of physical touch in my fifteen years as a priest and even more before that. God knows my parents never offered me affection, and I never enjoyed my romantic relationships with women—however fleeting they may have been, making the decision to become a priest—to flee a life of disparity and sin—an easy choice.

I can't deny that I've had thoughts, carnal heated thoughts that creep through me when I least expect it. God tests his strongest soldiers, and I'm not spared from temptation.

Seminary school challenged me for multiple reasons. Late night study sessions, lack of sleep, or time to eat, but a darker need presented itself to me. Images of naked flesh intertwined with mine. Men and women piqued these primal interests, and I found it hard to keep my thoughts at bay or my hands away from the pounding need between my legs.

Laurent and I had been roommates in school. He came from a well-off family in the South of France. He was born in America to an American family but had spent most of his life dripping with culture, fine wine, and a loving family surrounding him on the sandy shores of Nice. It puzzled me how he ended up in seminary school, not that I believed Priesthood was only fit for men who lived a bleak life, but Laurent seemed to have it all—money, dashing good looks, a loving family. He could have gotten married and lived a life surrounded by love without ever feeling the sting of loneliness. He'd said that despite everything his rich life had to offer, there was always something missing—a purpose his life seemed to lack. He'd never felt so complete until he started seminary school and became my roommate.

We found ourselves in precarious situations more than once. We'd never talked about it out loud, but now, laying in the grass and letting my mind drift to wherever it chooses to land, I can't help but think about one of those nights when it was dark and quiet, but the air was thick with something you can't name. My mind raced with images of mouths on skin, the sound of thrusting in and out of dark and delicious places. My hand found its way around my throbbing cock, trying my best to be quiet as I rubbed myself desperately.

Laurent was always a light sleeper, and when I heard rustling coming from his bed, only a few feet away from mine, I couldn't help but divert my gaze to him, staring back at me, eyes dark and intent, as his hands hid under his blankets moving up and down. His lips parted, and soft moans escaped him. I should have stopped then. Apologized, confessed my sins to my priest, and requested we separate as roommates, but I didn't. I didn't stop. I kept my eyes locked with his, jerking myself off until we both finished and closed our eyes around the euphoria–never opening them until the next morning.

It only happened a handful of times, and once we graduated, we both got a position at this countryside parish up in the mountains and far away from civilization. We had our own rooms and never found ourselves in that sinful situation ever again. The road to godliness isn't always straight and narrow; at least, that's what I tell my patrons. I just needed time to grow into my destiny—here at this parish with my best friend. My life is peaceful and full of joy. Even if sometimes still in the dead of night, I can't help but admit that my mind wanders, but I can keep those thoughts at bay now. I don't need to act on them.

A crow caws nearby, snapping my eyes open and bringing awareness to my hand, intertwined with Laurent's. I sit up, pulling my hand away and startling the sleeping Laurent beside me. "I better get to the kitchen. These vegetables aren't going to come to life and make themselves useful." I stand, brushing the grass off my slacks.

Laurent smiles and puts his hands behind his head, revealing the veiny underside of his muscled arms. He grins up at me, the light reflecting in his hazel eyes, the wind blowing through his golden hair. I imagine God crafted him in the image of his most beloved angel. His face is so chiseled that sometimes I want to reach out and touch it just to make sure it's real and not made of marble.

"Maybe if we pray hard enough, God will make our produce come to life and cook itself." He smiles.

"That would creep me the fuck out. Instead, let's just pray that this new cook coming tomorrow is decent."

"Decent?" Laurent sits up. "I'm praying for more than that. Ye of little faith. My God is bigger than the Boogeyman

. He will deliver us the most amazing cook that's ever walked this earth. That's how big my faith in Him is." I extend my hand and pull him to his feet, ignoring the warmness spreading through my body from the contact.

"Don't test God, Laurent. Fucked up things happen when people do that."

3

Emily

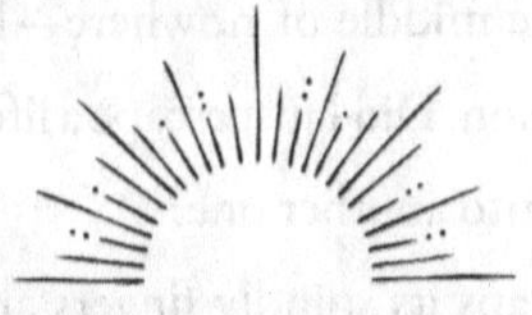

My arm hurts from pinching myself every time I remember I scored my dream position. Some little girls dream of being a veterinarian or a doctor, and maybe I had similar dreams once upon a time, but since the harsh world showed itself to me, my dream is to be surrounded by nature and live a peaceful, quiet life.

It should be a bit of a red flag that I got hired over the phone without being asked to show references or any proof of culinary expertise, but I'm too excited to care. I did have the where-with-all to ask why the position was available, and the woman, Gail, told me because the old cook left unexpectedly. Finding a replacement willing to work in such an isolated area had been a struggle for them. If I had any friends to share the news of my new job opportunity with, I'm sure they'd tell me this is a recipe for a horror movie disaster, but thanks to Darrell,

I lost all of those. So, no voices of reason for me. Only my own loud hope blaring that this will all work out.

As I walk down the desolate dirt road, three miles from where the city bus dropped me off, I raise my phone overhead, attempting to catch a signal. Maybe I didn't think everything through. I'm *really* off the grid, which sounded great, but now that I'm lost in the middle of nowhere—I'm starting to second-guess my decision. Did I just escape a life-threatening living situation to jump into another one?

Just as panic wraps its spindly fingers around my throat, a squatty cluster of stone buildings comes into view as I reach the top of a hill. I sigh in relief, my shoulders relaxing and my fingers tightening around the handles of my two suitcases. I pick up my pace, charging toward my new home.

A white-haired woman steps outside the door nearest the road. "Hello!" she calls enthusiastically as she waves. I wave back, unable to hide my grin as I take in my surroundings—rolling green hills, lush lines of produce, white linens hanging to dry, wooden chicken coop condos—it's a storybook come to life.

"I'm Gail, the Parish Administrator. You must be Emily," she yells when she's only a few paces ahead of me. She wears a long green skirt that falls to her ankles. Her white hair is tied behind her head, and she sports a wide, friendly grin across her wrinkle-strewn face. I pictured her in a nun uniform when I spoke to her on the phone. It settles my nerves that there's another employee here who isn't a nun or a priest—like maybe I will fit in after all.

I drop my bags at my feet and shake her outstretched hand. "Hi! It's nice to meet you. This place is so beautiful."

She places her hands on her hips and looks around, the sun catching the gold flakes in her hazel eyes. "Yes, God's splendor truly does dwell in this place."

I nod with a smile, clamming up a bit. Of course, I knew I'd be employed by a Catholic church, and everyone I'd be working alongside would be all religious and shit. Still, it's not until this moment that I realize I don't know anything about Catholicism. I don't know how to speak the language to fit in, and I don't know if they'd still want me to work for them if they knew I was a dirty heathen destined for hell. This feels like my first test, and I rack my brain for a response. "Praise be," I mutter, stumbling over the two words.

Gail squints an eye and looks at me. She laughs. "Was that the first time you've ever said that?"

My cheeks beat red, and my heart rate increases. "Maybe." So long dream job.

She studies me for a long moment before laughing and slapping my back. "You don't need to pretend to be something you're not here. Sure, we're a rural catholic church and look old-fashioned, but we're not as stuffy as we look." She winks.

"Oh, thank God," I say with a sigh of relief.

"There ya go. You even got God in that one. You'll fit in just fine."

She grabs my bags from me. I resist a bit, unsure if a woman her age can carry my luggage, but when she pulls back, revealing her impressive strength, I let go of my bags and allow the kind gesture. "Follow me," she says. "I'll show you around."

I take one last look at the beautiful nature around me before following Gail into the stone building. I take a big breath, feeling the fresh air refill my lungs and cleanse my nerves. Maybe I am the main character at the start of a rom-com. I'm not interested in flinging myself into a romance at the moment—probably not for a while after everything I've gone through, but maybe in a year or two, I could meet a sexy farmer, and my life would be my own. Hope feels sticky and sweet on my fingertips—a sensation I'd almost forgotten.

"Here's the kitchen," Gail says as we make our way through the wooden doorway. "You'll have free range in here. You can find your produce and seasonings in the garden. You'll have to make a list of other items you need in town. We get meats and other essentials delivered once a week."

I nod, swiveling my head to register the rustic room around me. A butcher-block island sits in the middle of the space. White cabinets and stainless-steel appliances line the cream-blue walls. Birds chirp through the opened window over the sink, and plants drape over the high surfaces. "This is great!" I say, unable to contain my excitement.

"I think so too. I'd love for this to be my workspace, but sadly, I only know how to make a mediocre grilled cheese." She walks toward the other side of the room. "You should find all the cooking utensils you need in the drawers and cabinets, but let me know if you need anything else."

I nod, not mentioning that I haven't even owned a cheese grater in my adult life. I imagine I can more than make do with whatever utensils are provided.

"Let me show you to your room," she says, turning to the room closest to the kitchen. It's simple—white walls, a dark wooden bedframe holding a full-sized mattress, a blue quilt folded on the end of the bed. A matching dresser rests against the wall, and two end tables sit on either side of the bed. Light spills through the open window, shadows dancing across the walls from the swaying sheer curtains. "It's not much, but hopefully, you'll be comfortable."

"It's perfect." I can't mask my giddy smile. It's clean and safe and all mine. I couldn't ask for anything more.

Gail smiles at me—warmness and a knowing look in her eyes. "Great."

Muffled laughing streams from a room across the hall. "Oh, that must be the priests. They'll be the people you're primarily cooking for. They're the only other people that live here full-time. It doesn't sound like they're too busy. Let me introduce you." She knocks twice on the wooden door before someone yells to open it from the other side. She cracks it open and sticks her head in. "Emily, the new cook, is here."

"Yay!" someone exclaims.

"Send her in," says another voice.

Gail opens the door wide and steps to the side. I stare across the threshold into the office. A large oak desk rests parallel to me. On the other side sits a well-built man with curly brown hair, dark and haunting brown eyes, a strong jaw, and wearing a black shirt with the quintessential priestly collar. Sitting on the edge of the desk is a another man with dirty-blonde, shaggy hair tucked behind his ears. He's tall and not as stocky as the other man but fit. His green and yellow speckled eyes shine through the room like a mythical beacon. Both of them look to be in their late twenties or early thirties.

They study me intently—thick silence silencing us and seeming to last for an eternity. Finally, it's broken. "Hello, I'm Father Robert," says the man sitting behind the desk.

I gulp, my muscles freezing around my bones.

"And I'm Father Laurent."

Father. Fuck me. I knew there would be priests, but *hot* priests? What kind of rom-com is this?

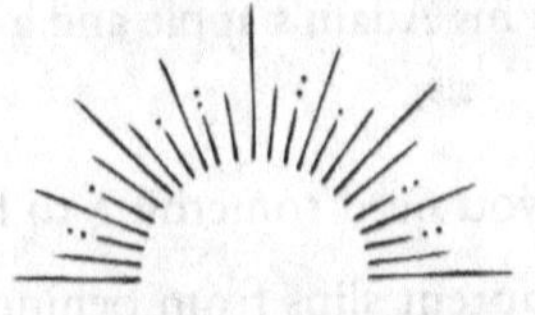

4
Emily

I don't remember the last time I've been in a church, but as I sit in the wooden pews facing the elaborate stained-glass window above the lonely pulpit, memories swirl all around me. It feels unnatural, but I know what to do: flip down the long stool before me, kneel, bring my hands to my face, and close my eyes. I've seen enough movies.

Thankfully, I'm here by myself because I need to get these words out loud. I can't just say them in my head. I've always been a yapper. "Hey God, it's me, Emily. I know it's been a while since I talked to you. Actually, I don't know if I ever talked to you or even believe in you. Anyway, I'm just here to chat and beg you to give me some direction in life as I start this new chapter. I want to let you know I'm open to whatever life you have for me." A horrible thought pops into my head. "On second thought, I really don't want to be a nun. Don't get me wrong, the outfits are sick, and I'm totally down with the eternal female friendship bit. I just need a little dick every now and then. You understand, right?"

"We most definitely understand."

My blood solidifies in my veins, and I shoot my eyes open. Father Robert stands before me, dressed in an all black robe. A white collar covers his Adam's apple and a rosary hangs to his chest.

"You look like you need something to fill that hole inside of you." Father Laurent slips from behind Father Robert in matching attire. Both of their faces are stern—authoritative, but their words feel different—suggestive and loose.

I attempt to pick myself up from my knees. "Oh, I'm sorry. I thought I was alone."

Father Robert extends a hand, holding me back down to the stool. "Don't get up." He grabs my chin, bringing my gaze to his dark and heated eyes. "You are perfect right where you are."

I gulp loud enough that it echoes through the wooden, empty room.

Father Laurent walks around and down the pew until he reaches me, placing a large hand on my shoulder. "Don't look so nervous. You asked God to fill you up, and here we are—ready to use you for His will." He presses against me, his large erection hitting my arm through his black slacks. Desire swims through my senses. I'm thoroughly embarrassed, and I can't tell if the two mean the suggestive words that come from them, but I can't help but feel the warmth rushing to my core. I didn't even know I had a priest kink, but goddamn is this hot as fuck.

Father Robert applies pressure to my mouth, forcing my jaw to snap open. "Are you ready to take what the Lord orders of you?"

My eyes water from his fingertips, still digging into my jaw. I don't move, though—waiting for what happens next. Father Robert reaches for his belt, moving slowly as he undoes his pants. I can't turn my head to look at Father Laurent, but I hear the jiggling of his belt buckle and feel something warm and hard slap against my arm.

"Grab him," Father Robert says, his hand down his pants, not revealing himself to me yet.

I don't hesitate, doing as I'm told. I gasp once my fingers attempt to wrap around Father Laurent. He's hard—so hard, unlike any cock I've felt before. He's also smooth. Almost like a...I don't know, a cucumber? I break free from Father Robert's grasp and turn my head. Sure enough, a firm and green cucumber juts from where Father Laurent's cock should be. My mouth waters. Instead of being disturbed, I'm completely aroused. The cool air teases my bare nipples, pebbling them even more. Wait, my bare nipples? I look down and sure enough, I'm stark naked.

***

I jolt up from my bed. My breath heavy, and my heart racing as I assess the dark room around me. I'm not in a church sanctuary with two hot priests cornering me like I'm prey to be devoured. No, I'm in my room, covered in sweat and an insatiable need pounding between my legs. It was a dream, a sexy, weird, and totally inappropriate dream.

"Fuck!" I mutter. Falling back down and pulling my pillow over my head. It's only the first night. How I'm I supposed to thrive here when I'm already having fucked up thoughts about my employers? I guess technically, God's my employer? But I don't think he'd be too happy about me wanting to fuck his pure, shining, golden boys.

When I met Father Robert and Laurent, I barely said ten words. My throat clogged up, and I was sure if I stood in their presence for much longer, I might pass out. I'm not usually like this—so boy crazy that my blood pressure plummets. Maybe it's the feeling of safety after escaping an abusive relationship. Maybe it's the fact that they're priests. I may not know a lot about Catholicism, but I do know priests are married to God and are never allowed to be in a romantic relationship. Maybe my trauma has rewired my brain to be magnetically attracted to men I know won't hurt me because I can't even have them. Or, maybe, and probably the most likely, Father Robert and Father Laurent are two of the hottest men I've ever seen. How dickish of them to resign to a life of celibacy with looks like that. It's just selfish, honestly.

I clamp my eyes shut and count my breaths, trying to will myself to fall back asleep. The images of Father Robert's heated eyes sear into my brain. The feeling of Father Laurent's cucumber cock in my hand still warms my skin. Why did I imagine his cock as a cucumber? Fuck, if I know. Maybe it was my brain's weird way of letting me know I need some refreshments. I abandon my attempts at sleep and pop out of bed, putting on my slippers and tip-toeing out my bedroom door. It's like I'm a teenager, breaking the rules and sneaking in the cabinets for a midnight snack. I straighten my spine once I remember Gail telling me the kitchen is my domain. I'm the head cook, after all. If I want to make a midnight snack of chopped cucumbers, I'm doing it.

It's dark in the kitchen; the only source of light is an almost full moon outside the window above the sink. I stumble, feeling around the wall until I find the light switch. I scream. Father Laurent, now visible, sits at the island in the middle of the kitchen, eating a bowl of cereal. "Boo," he whispers with a smile, milk dripping down the corner of his lips. He wears a white T-shirt and navy blue sleep pants. I will my eyes not to scan him more, eager but scared to notice his frame outside of his priest outfit.

"I'm so sorry," I whisper in between labored breaths. My hand is placed over my beating heart as I will my nerves to settle. I'm never falling back to sleep. This is too much excitement for one night.

He rolls his shoulders and puts down his bowl, bringing his long finger to his chin. "Why are you sorry?"

"I didn't mean to disturb you. I didn't know anyone was in here."

"This is your kitchen. Besides, I was sitting in the dark like a weirdo. I'm the one who should be sorry."

He's right, of course, but this is my first night, and he's lived here much longer. I can't help but feel like the one intruding. But the casual cadence of his voice and his comfortable posture at his stool makes me feel more at ease.

"Did you also come for a midnight snack?" he asks.

"Yeah, I did, but I'm okay. You can keep eating. I'll be fine until the morning."

"Nonsense." He pulls out the stool next to him. "Grab yourself a bowl and join me. I'd love to get to know you better. We didn't have much time after our first introduction."

I think of my swift exit and awkward greeting after meeting the priests for the first time and cringe. I do need to redeem myself, but this is a bad idea. Of course, I will be around the priests quite a bit, but after the dream I just awoke from, I think I should keep my distance. But what am I supposed to do now—while he stares at me with those magnetic eyes and that boyish grin on his face? How can I say no? Besides, he's a man of God. Even if the sinful thoughts got the best of me, it's not like anything would actually happen.

"Okay," I say before walking toward the cabinets, pulling out a white-ceramic bowl, and bringing it to the island where a glass jug of milk and the cardboard box of Reese's Puffs already sits. It's not the chopped cucumber I had in mind, but it's for the best. I should probably keep my distance from cucumbers for a little while. I smile and shake my head as I pour the brown balls into my bowl, trying my best to ignore Father Laurent's searing stare.

"What?" he asks.

"I just haven't had these since I was a kid."

"Well, that's just sad."

It's odd. He doesn't talk like I'd expect a priest to sound. He's young, but he's a man of God. I figured he'd sound as formal as a grandpa.

I walk over to the other side of the counter, taking the seat next to him. "Never thought to buy it at the store."

"That's the whole point of being an adult. You get to buy all the junk food your parents limited whenever you want."

I take a big bite, feeling the tingles of nostalgia in the peanut butter taste. "Except when you're an adult, you can't just use your parent's wallet to buy things, and now you have to worry about shit like your health." It takes a second for me to realize I just cursed. "Shit!" I clamp my hand over my mouth.

"What is happening right now?" Father Laurent says as he leans closer, studying my face with his spoon pointed at me.

"I'm sorry! I didn't mean to say that."

"Say what?"

Maybe he hadn't heard it. "The bad word. Don't worry, it won't happen again."

He laughs, taking another spoonful of his cereal. "You don't need to worry about that here. I'd watch it a little bit more when you're in front of the patrons, but you don't need to pretend you're something you're not in front of us."

"But isn't cursing a sin? Doesn't it offend you?" I haven't been around a lot of religious people, but I assumed it was a no-no.

"It's just a word, Emily." My name sounds like warm brown sugar on his tongue. He says it like he held the word in his mouth and savored it before giving it back to me. Something heavy swims through me, and I must shake slightly to bring myself back to the moment.

He goes on. "Words are just words. It's the actions that matter." He brings another spoonful of cereal to his mouth, keeping his eyes on mine as a drop of milk falls from the corner of his mouth, and he quickly cleans it up with his knuckle.

I advert my gaze back to the bowl in front of me, twirling around the brown balls and darkening the milk. I don't feel hungry anymore. "That makes sense."

"Are you a religious person?" he asks.

I tense. Surprisingly, no one has asked me this during my short interview process. I'd figured it would come up by now, and I have been dreading the moment I'd have to answer. I love this place and I would say anything to stay, but the truth will come up. I can't even go a few minutes without swearing in front of the priests. I breathe out. "I haven't been, but honestly, at this point in my life, I'm looking for something. Something that makes sense. Something that gives me purpose."

He chuckles, warm and low. "That's exactly how I felt when I joined the ministry."

"Really?" I turn to him. I think about my prayer in my dream. I still do not want to become a nun, and hopefully, my search for purpose in a parish will not end with my celibacy.

"I mean, obviously, I took it to the extreme," he says as if reading my mind. I study his tanned face, hazel eyes, and chiseled bone structures. There has to be more to the story. He's so beautiful. How could someone like him choose this kind of life? But who am I to judge?

I'm so lost in my thoughts that I barely notice the thick silence that has rolled over us. Father Laurent stares at my lips as if waiting to see when they'll move next. It's suddenly much too warm in this kitchen.

"Well, I should get back to bed. Big first day making my new bosses breakfast."

"I'm not your boss, Emily." There's my name again, sounding dirty on his lips.

"Then what are you?"

"Your co-worker, your Father." He smiles.

Did he just make a joke? A weird joke? I stand, picking up my bowl. "Let's stick with co-workers. I already have enough issues with my actual father."

"Right, let's stick with that. Oh, shit, is that the time?" he says, looking at the digital clock over the oven.

"Yeah, I know it's pretty late." I stop. "Wait a second. Did you just say shit?"

"Oops." He puts his fingers over his grin, and his eyes widen. "Am I already a bad influence?"

He laughs. "No, don't worry. I've always had a dirty mouth."

My skin pricks. "A priest with a dirty mouth?"

"Oh, Emily, I promise Father Robert and I are nothing like the priests you're used to."

I think he means it light-heartedly, as if they're just two young guys keeping it cool, but I sense a hint of flirtation in his voice, as if he's ready to show me just *how* different he can be. No, absolutely not. I shake my head and walk toward the hallway out of the kitchen. "Well, goodnight, Father Laurent."

"Sweet dreams, Emily," he calls after me. There's no way he could know what I woke up from, but goddamn, does it feel like he can read me better than a Bible.

5

Laurent

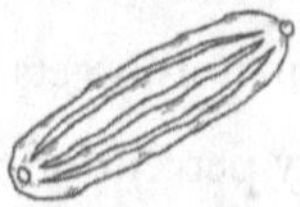

"And that, my friends, is an example of how great our God's love is for us. We are not worthy of his grace, and yet time and time again, he washes away our sins with his blood," Robert says, closing the leather-bound notebook atop the podium.

I sit on the wooden chair on stage beside him. We take turns delivering the sermon. One week, it's Robert; the next, mine. It's not a typical arrangement, but when the parish hired us many years ago, they thought it would be a good way to get us settled into our roles. It turns out that the congregation loves the switch-up of our delivery styles and having two priests instead of one. No one has asked one of us to move churches or step down, and Robert and I can't complain—especially me.

I could watch Robert speak for the rest of my days—the way his dark eyes narrow in on an invisible point at the back of the congregation, his strong and delicate hand tense around his notes, his side profile illuminated by the stage lights. Whenever it's my turn to speak, though, I revel in the knowledge that Robert sits where I am now—watching me, and sometimes I like to imagine the same thoughts I have rush through him at the sight of me.

"Now, let us stand and sing, Holy God, We Praise Thy Name." The congregation noisily gets to their feet, breaking me out of my trance. Ninety percent of our patrons are widowed women above the age of sixty. We hear the whispers at the monthly potlucks; they're here for one reason and one reason alone, and it's not to share knitting secrets. It doesn't matter that we're betrothed to God and the ages of some of their grandsons—these women like their young masculine eye candy. I don't blame them. Hell, they're here for the same reason I am.

I rise, belting out the notes I could sing in my sleep, my eyes never leaving Robert. He closes his eyes as if the congregation's voice tucks him into an ethereal hug.

He's the real deal, unlike me, who's faking it most of the time. He's always been that way. In seminary school, I was in awe of him, even more so than I am now. He didn't have any questions–only answers. It felt like God spoke to him like his closest confidant. I was jealous at first. Why him and not me? But I quickly learned that jealousy wasn't that at all. I didn't want to be him. I just wanted him, all of him.

I came to seminary school to find my purpose. Life was always fun–always easy, but there was something missing. My uncle had been a priest, and my family spoke of him with the most esteemed honor. I was nineteen with no direction. I thought I'd fuck around at seminary school and find out if the Catholic church had all the answers they always proclaim to have. It felt just like Emily described last night—an attempt to find my purpose. I was lost, just like her searching for something, and boy, did I find it. If only I knew the God of my attention would stir more in me than I ever thought possible.

The celibacy thing actually wasn't an issue. I'd had my fair share of pussy in my early years, and it always disappointed me. It was so meaningless, so fast, missing something entirely. Those few nights with Robert, with just my hand, his labored breaths, and my mind, did more for me than any of my previous sexual experiences. Of course, something was missing, always something missing.

The song ends, and I snap myself out of my thoughts. I'll need to return to my quarters and take care of myself before lunch. I thank God daily for my strong hand and my healthy imagination. Priests aren't supposed to jack themselves off, I know, but I have a looser interpretation of the Bible. Why would God give me these needs if I shouldn't act on them? It's not like it's hurting anyone. Sometimes, when I'm stroking myself and Robert's face comes to mind, it's like God sent it to me himself.

My self-pleasure isn't as frequent as I'd like. The walls are thin. But I couldn't control myself after talking to Emily last night. After she left the kitchen, I wobbled back to my room, hard and throbbing, thankful that our conversation didn't last longer, so my inappropriate thoughts didn't take hold of me. Her plump lips, her wide eyes, her breasts pushing against her thin sleep t-shirt—it had all been too much. And then when she opened her mouth—God dammit. She was funny, and talking to her felt easy. She was nervous and flustered in my presence, something I'm used to from the older women here, but never with someone who looks like her—who smells and sounds like her.

It was a relief, one I praised the Lord for, that after all these years of wanking to Robert, a fresh face came to mind. Instead of imagining myself taking his dick in my mouth, his warm come running down my throat, I imagined myself with my face between her breasts, suffocating me as I pumped in and out of her sweet and tight cunt. I'd come fast and thought it could hold me off for a few days. Maybe my obsession with Robert was sated. But nope, all it took was one look from him this morning as he stumbled out of his room across from mine—his hair a mess and his eyes half hooded. God, I wanted to push him back into his room and kiss the sleep off his face.

"Go in peace to love and serve the Lord," Robert says, the congregation responding with an "amen." He turns to me. "Could you tell I made half that shit up on the spot?" he whispers, leaning in.

"Not at all, dear boy," I say, gently slapping his chin. I never miss an opportunity to touch his skin. After fifteen years of pining for this man, I might be so far into my delusion, but sometimes, I swear my touch elicits a visceral response from him, even as he tries to hide it.

We make our way off the stage, outside the pews, and to the chapel doors to say goodbye to our patrons. The women stall, chatting with other big-hatted ladies until we're at our post at the entrance. We barely get a second to breathe before they line up, ready to shake our hands and banter.

"Thank you for coming," I say, grabbing Ms. Gardenia's wrinkled hand.

"I'll never miss a Sunday service! Might I mention that you boys look rather frail? I heard you lost your cook. How about I come over sometime this week and cook you a proper dinner?"

"That is kind of you, but we actually just hired a new cook." As if sent by angels, I catch a glimpse of Emily's glossy brown hair poking behind the aisle of grays. "And here she is!" I say, stepping to the side to catch Emily's eyes.

"Sorry," she mouths to the women staring her down as she scoots past to get closer to me. She stands just inches away, her earthy and lavender smell pulling me in. Her eyes dart, and she tucks a strand of hair behind her ears before reaching up on her tip-toes so I can hear her soft words. "I'm sorry, I was just going to wait until you both were finished. Lunch is ready. I didn't know when to have it ready or when you two normally eat. It's soup, so it will probably get cold, but I can always heat it up." Nerves radiate from her words. It occurs to me that no one has filled her in on her schedule or given her any orientation. I feel like a dick.

I reach out, grabbing her upper arm. "It's okay. We'll be there in just a moment. You've timed it perfectly." I smile at her and watch as a bright color warms her cheeks. She's so responsive to my words. Blood rushes to my groin, and I angle my legs and pull away from her.

"Okay, great," she says, her eyes shifting to Robert's next to me. I watch as he detaches from his conversation with Ms. Fran. His eyes catching hers in a thick stare. Emily's cheeks redden even more before she pushes back through the crowd and disappears.

I study Robert, now back to his conversation. Maybe I'm reading him wrong. Maybe he senses something between Emily and me and is weary of what's to come. I can't be sure, but something was in that look he gave her. His hands clench at his side, his veins thick.

"Oh, Father Laurent. I have something for you!" Ms. Manatez grabs my attention, popping in front of me with a baby-blue knitted pile in her hands. "The weather is starting to chill, and I didn't want you to catch a cold all the way up this hill."

I grab the fabric from her, bringing it up to my line of vision and straightening it out. It's a beautiful sweater. Perfectly knitted with a yellow duck in the middle. Odd choice, but I can't deny that it is very much me. "Oh, Barbara Manatez, you are the one for me!" I exclaim, wrapping the old woman into a friendly hug.

She giggles like a schoolgirl, blushing and barely able to form a sentence before she scampers off.

Robert leans over once she leaves. "You can't be talking to these women like that. You're encouraging them," he scolds. I love it when I get him angry. His furrowed brows, his serious eyes. God, it sends a jolt through my body.

I hold up the sweater with a shit-eating grin. "You're just jealous that no one is knitting you a sweater."

He examines it. "Yeah, so jealous," he says with an eye roll.

The sanctuary is empty now, and Robert and I start to close the large ten-foot wooden doors. Before we shut them completely, a frail voice sounds behind us. "I don't think you'd want me trapped in here with you boys."

I startle, turning to meet the old woman dressed in a dark cloak. A large boil sits upon her crooked nose, and she smiles up at me with a gapped-tooth grin. My heart hammers in my chest, and I'm unable to find words. Luckily, Robert finds his first. "I'm so sorry, ma'am. We didn't realize anyone else was in here with us."

She waves a frail hand in dismissal. "No bother. I have a way of sneaking around to get the best views." She looks us up and down with a knowing smile.

I stall, wondering what she's implying. "I don't think we've had the pleasure. I'm Father Laurent." I extend my hand.

She eyes my offering but returns her gaze up to my eyes. "I know who you are." She looks at Robert. "I know who you both are, probably better than you know yourselves."

Robert and I exchange a look. We've had our fair share of patrons losing their marbles right before our eyes.

Robert clears his throat and steps forward. "Can I give you a ride home, ma'am?"

She laughs, a screeching sound. "I can take care of myself. You two, though, you both need some help."

Yep, definitely lost her marbles. I nod and smile. "Alright, ma'am. Thanks so much for coming. Hope to see you next week." I open the door enough for her to exit.

She walks past us and through the now-cleared entryway. Robert and I exchange an eye roll and a smile. When I return my gaze to the woman, I startle. She stands right before me, eyes glued to mine. "Tonight is the Harvest Moon, where spirits come to play. All that is hidden will be brought to light. You two need a transformation. It's up to you both to define the true fruits of your soul."

She pulls the tail of her cloak around her, turning in a dramatic fashion before scurrying down the walkway, away from the church.

"What the fuck?" Robert says slowly, turning to me with a laugh. "This is what I'm talking about, Laurent. We can't encourage these women. Some of them are just seconds away from losing their minds."

My heart beats in my chest, and I don't take my eyes off the woman as she grows smaller and winds down the hills. Robert's casual words pull me back into the moment. I'm not one to scare easily, but something about that woman spooked the crap out of me.

I part my lips. "Barbara Manatez is a saint. Reminds me of my nan."

"I hope your nan didn't want to fuck you because Ms. Manatez definitely wants to fuck you."

Fuck. I *definitely* need to jerk myself before lunch. Watching Robert's lips curl around the syllables I've dreamed about him moaning into my ear—it's too much. I shake my head, searching for a response that masks my thoughts. I jog in front of him, turning to face him as I pull the duck sweater over my head. "You might have a point. This duck sweater is rather sexy."

"Boo!" He shouts, cupping his mouth with his hands.

"Ah, come on. This doesn't do it for you?" I spin slowly.

He runs up to me and pushes me. "Ya, you wish."

I chuckle, biting my tongue, because fuck yeah. I absolutely wish.

Robert

Sometimes, in the dead of night, the quietness of the countryside is too loud. I toss and turn, the bellowing of frogs, the wind whooshing through trees, the creaks of the old floorboards—all of it melts together to prevent me from any sort of sleep. It becomes too much, and I jump to my feet, heading toward the kitchen and searching through the cupboards. I'm usually an excellent sleeper. Not even a tornado could wake me, but this time is different because *she's* sleeping in the room down the hall.

I thought hiring a new cook would give me time to focus on the Lord's word, but ever since Emily showed up at my office door two days ago, I've been more distracted than a teenager shopping with his mom at a lingerie store.

There's something about her. Her smell, her nervous laugh, the way her eyes dart whenever I focus my attention on her—it all elicits a visceral reaction from me. I make her nervous, it's obvious. She's conventionally attractive—long brown hair, unblemished skin, a sprinkle of freckles, and a curtain of bangs right above her chocolate brown eyes. Any man would take notice of her, except I'm not any man. I'm a man of God. Plenty of beautiful women have been in my presence without heightening my blood pressure to a single degree, but there's something different about her—something I can't name.

And then there's the way Laurent responds to her. He's a devilish flirt with the older women in the congregation, but it always seemed like part of a bit. The way he acts with her—well, it reminds me of how he behaves with me. Cheeky, smiley, his eyes examining one piece of her at a time. I'm not sure if it's jealousy or my mind playing tricks on me, but I've never eaten so fast as I have during the last three meals with the two of them.

I've run into Emily on her own in the hall. She nearly jumped out of her skin, picking at her fingernails and staring down at her toes. It took every ounce of my reserve not to grab her chin and pull her attention toward me. It's like something in me knows what she needs—direction, stability, someone to take control. Why the fuck do I know that? Why the fuck do I want that person to be me?

Being around her alone is too much. Being around her and Laurent at the same time—actual torture. My skin becomes too hot. My blood pumps too thick for my heart, and I must remove myself to catch my breath.

Maybe this is a test from God. I blamed my distraction on the missing cook. Now we have a replacement, and I'm even worse off. I shouldn't have excuses. I should be able to give God my full attention regardless of my situation. I need to pray—longer and harder than I've ever prayed, but right now, I need a fucking drink.

I continue my search through the top cabinets until I find the old bottle of communion wine I saved for a rainy day. "Thank you, Lord," I whisper as I yank the cork off and take a giant swig from the bottle. The liquid runs down my throat, immediately giving me a fraction of relief. But it's not enough. My mind still jitters, and my hands shake like a negative charge, desperate to get to the positive under my sleep pants.

I need to get out of this house. They're too close. I need to be alone with God. I step out into the night, cringing when the kitchen door shuts louder than I anticipated. I trudge through the rows of produce until I find a good spot between the tomato and cucumber crops. The moon shines an odd orange glow overhead, and I stare at it quizzically as I make myself comfortable, propping my head up with my arms as I continue drinking my wine.

It doesn't take long for the wine to lighten things around me, and I breathe in relief. My hands still shake, though, and it's like my cock is another entity entirely—the devil begging me to take hold. It would work—jerking myself off. I'd feel relief, but it wouldn't last long. It wouldn't be worth the Hail Marys later.

"God, why is this happening to me?" I ask out loud into the noisy woodland night around me.

"You have been disobedient," a deep voice responds.

"What?" I pop up into a seated position, looking around the field.

"Yes, very disobedient. To amend your sins, you must obey every command of your brother, Laurent."

"Oh, fuck off!" I yell, noticing his voice and a rustle from a corn stalk a few feet away.

Laurent emerges from the brush, bent over in laughter.

"Leave me alone!" I yell, falling back to the earth and swinging my arm over my eyes to hide my misery.

"Oh, come on," Laurent says between his laughter, stumbling over to me. "Don't be mad at me. Why are you banging around in the kitchen if you didn't want me to follow you out here?"

"I wasn't banging around." The door did shut harder than I anticipated, but I wonder if Laurent struggles to sleep as much as I am.

"You certainly woke me up." He plops down on the ground next to me, reaching over me for the bottle of wine. He's too close already, and the warmth of his body seeps through my pores. I scoot over, still annoyed with him, but hand the wine to him anyway.

"What are you doing out here?" he asks.

"Clearly, I came alone to talk to God."

"Ah, but aren't you so glad I answered instead?" he asks before chugging the red wine. A drop falls down his chin, barely illuminated by the light of the orange moon.

"No. I'd rather the devil answer."

"I'm sure you would, you sadist fuck," he says, pushing me before shoving the bottle back into my hand. "What are you begging God for anyway? What troubles you?" He lies on his side, his head propped up with his arm as he stares at me.

I glance at him from the corner of my eye, the sight of him making my blood pump strangely. I return my attention to the dark field before me. "I've been distracted."

"I thought not having to cook your own meals was the solution."

"Apparently, it's not. It seems to be getting worse."

"Ah, probably because the new cook has a pair of amazing tits."

"Laurent!" I yell, slapping his arm and glancing around as if someone will overhear us. We never censor our talk around each other, but we're priests. We don't discuss attraction in such a way. His words cross a line we've never touched. Maybe we've tip-toed close, but it's never been said so openly.

He sighs as if exhausted. "Oh, don't act so holy. I see the way you look at her. You're a man, Robert. I don't judge."

"I'm not just a man. I'm a man of God."

"Even God was tempted during the forty days and forty nights."

I ponder for a moment, examining him from the corner of my eyes. He does have a point. It's not a sin to be distracted. It's not a sin to want to thrust my cock so deep into Emily's throat until she gags around me, calling me her God, worshiping me as I ring the moisture from her heavenly cunt. It's not even a sin to wish Laurent was there too—to have them both take turns running their tongues from my tip to my base. No, it's not a sin at all. Maybe this isn't a test. Maybe this is a lesson—to show me what a common person dreams of. I can be strong. I can withstand temptation—no matter how hard. And right now, I'm definitely hard.

"I'm right, aren't I?" Laurent asks after I haven't responded for several minutes.

"No, you're not right."

He gasps. "Father, are you lying to me?"

"It's not her tits. It's her lips that drive me crazy."

Laurent pops up to a seated position, screeching into a laugh. "There you are, my boy! That's what I like to hear—the truth." He slaps my arm, and I grab his hand, pulling him back down next to me. "Shut up! You're going to wake the whole town!"

He palms his mouth, turning to me with eyes creased in a watery laugh. "I'm sorry. I'm sorry," he whispers.

I can't help it. He's so joyous–so full of life. I shake my head, breaking out in a quiet laugh.

"What?" he asks, reaching behind him, pulling a cucumber from the vine, and bringing it to his lips before taking a loud, crunchy bite.

"You are ridiculous."

"Yes, but only because you love it." He pats my cheek. "My mission from God is to bring you joy."

I reach behind me, feeling for something to sink my teeth into. My fingers graze a tomato, ripe and firm. I bring it to my mouth and take a bite, mimicking Laurent. "What a simple life you live. Here I am, leading the lost souls to God while you laze about, making jokes about tits. You must be God's favorite."

Tomato juice drips down my chin, and Laurent reaches over to wipe it, laughing. "You're definitely God's favorite. He made me just to serve you."

I roll away from him and stare back up at the starry night sprinkled amongst the orange-hued sky. The wine has settled around me, making my limbs and eyelids heavy. I barely register my words, sleep winning the war on my consciousness. "If only you could truly serve me the way I choose."

Laurent murmurs something next to me, his voice as sleepy as mine, but I don't register his words—just drift off to a peaceful sleep.

7

Laurent

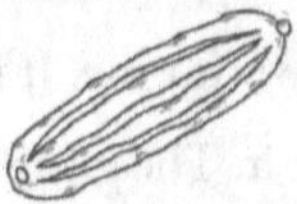

Sun kisses my skin, stirring me from my slumber. I'm in the garden. My mind races, filling in the gaps about how I ended up here. My body weighs me down, and I recall the bottle of wine Robert and I shared last night. We're lightweights. Priests don't drink often, so the eleven percent alcohol content sure affected us.

I don't move. Gathering my bearings as I stare up at the blue sky. Everything looks funny–almost like I'm in a carnival funhouse surrounded by mirrors, making me appear small. I'm not ready to deal with the day—to ponder the words Robert shared with me last night, to think about how close we slept next to each other, our bodies almost touching in the warm moonlight.

The ground shakes around me. My mind jumps to the conclusion of an earthquake. I don't think we have those here. I've never experienced them, but I could have been lucky. I try to push up, but I'm stuck—my body frozen. *What kind of wine was that?* I didn't think I was that drunk last night, but I'm completely incapacitated. I start to panic, trying with all my might to move as the ground shakes more violently.

I tell myself to breathe, but it's no use. Something moves above me, stealing all the oxygen from my lungs. It's a hand—a giant hand, reaching down for me. It's not until the fingertips grip my skin that I realize it. The giant isn't grabbing my skin at all. No, I don't have normal flesh anymore. My body is hard and firm. Oh my god, am I dead? Is my body already experiencing rigor mortis, and now I'm trapped in a lifeless corpse? Maybe this giant is a god, taking me to the afterlife. But then she brings me to her face, and I make her out.

It's a god, alright. It's Emily. Her deep brown eyes suck me in, and even as I panic, I can't help getting lost in them. She examines me, licking her lips. I almost don't care to dissect what the fuck is going on—too mesmerized by her intoxicating features until I catch my reflection in her eyes.

She's not holding a tiny version of me. She's holding a cucumber. A fucking cucumber. I'm a cucumber. It's almost too ridiculous to be a dream, but it has to be because what the fuck?

She shifts her attention to her other hand, and I glance over to see the tomato she's holding. As I look at the round, firm vegetable, something in me pings. That's not a tomato at all. That's Robert. I could recognize him in any form. It doesn't look like Robert. It looks like a goddamn tomato, but as much as I can tell I'm a cucumber, I can tell that tomato is Robert.

What was in that fucking wine? Did someone drug us? Who dreams about you and your best friend turning into produce? Maybe I need therapy. Do priests get therapy? Definitely not. Trauma is something God should be able to deal with. But I will need something extra whenever I wake up from this.

Emily shivers as if a sudden chill washed through her. She shakes her head. "What's wrong with me?" she whispers before placing Robert and me in a woven basket on the ground. We're dropped on top of potatoes, peppers, and a head of lettuce. I can tell right away the produce is just that—not other transformed priests. I don't know why I know that, but I do.

I stare up above, watching as the blue sky changes to the familiar ceiling of our kitchen. Emily places the basket on the countertop. I listen as she steps over to the cabinet and rummages through pots and pans. The sounds, the smells, and everything around me seem so real. Whenever I'm in a dream, I can't tell, but if I suspected I was in one, I'd start to notice the errors—the blurry edges. Everything around me is concrete. Unless it's the most immersive lucid dream I've ever experienced, this isn't a dream—this is real. I can't talk, and I can't move. I want to reach out to Robert to see if he's conscious like me, but I can do nothing.

Emily's angelic face appears above me—a large sharp knife in her hand. Oh my God. I was so concerned about living life as a sentient cucumber that I forgot the worst part of all—I'm food.

Emily's about to have her plump lips around me, except instead of my cock as I've dreamed about, it will be my entire body snapped under her molars. Maybe Robert was right. Maybe God is punishing us. Who knew he was such a sinister fuck?

To my relief, Emily places the knife down next to the basket before grabbing Robert and me in each of her hands. She brings us to her face, examining us closely. Her fingers gently dance around my body. I should be freaking out, but her touch sends a shiver through my cucumber frame. Not actually—I can't move, but internally, I feel hot and bothered. Her lips part, her breath heavies, and her eyelids droop. She brings me to her lips.

Fear doesn't take hold of me like it did when she held the knife. I don't care if she takes a giant bite out of me. God, do I want to be in her mouth, to feel her lips on my green skin. Maybe God isn't sinister; maybe he's giving me exactly what I want, except as a cucumber. Weird, but God is known for doing some weird shit. He did make a donkey talk to teach some poor chap a lesson.

"Oh my God," Emily whispers, her lips almost touching me.

Yes, I think to myself, *thank you, God.* It's been years since I've had a woman's mouth on me, and I'll take it, even as a cucumber. I'm not a priest anymore—not even a man. She can use me however she sees fit.

My journey to her lips stops, and Emily opens her eyes wide. "What the fuck is wrong with me?" she exclaims, her voice dripping in shame. She places us back down on the counter, gathering the rest of the produce and bringing it to a cutting board by the sink.

Without Emily so close to me, I can think properly. I thank the Lord that I'm still alive. We'll sort of—whatever the fuck this kind of life is. My mind wonders as I watch Emily cut the unlucky vegetables. Is she always so attracted to cucumbers? Maybe I'm not dead or in my own dream at all. Maybe Emily has a cucumber kink, and I'm somehow in her dream. Or maybe Emily feels something about us because she can sense we're not vegetables. Maybe if I try hard enough, I can reach out to her.

I spend the next few moments straining to do anything. It hurts my brain, but after ten minutes, I swear I'm able to move myself a fraction of an inch. It could be in my head, but I need any sort of hope right now. Maybe if I try hard enough, I can move more.

Emily finishes cutting the produce. She drops the knife and extends her arms, holding herself up on the counter in deep thought. She takes a sharp breath before turning to Robert and me on the counter. Shit, did I do something? Did I signal her attention?

She walks over to us, slowly and with a nervous expression. She takes a big gulp of air before picking us back up, examining us in each of her hands. "Maybe I just need a release. It's that weird dream I had," she whispers to us.

I'm too lost in her beauty to contemplate her words. It's like I can feel her thickening pulse through her touch. She glances over her shoulders before turning and walking to her bedroom door with us still in her grasp.

Her bedroom. We're going to her bedroom. I can understand the look on her face. She doesn't just want to eat me. She definitely wants me inside of her but in an entirely different place. Praise the Lord for whatever the heck is going on right now, because God do I fucking love being a cucumber.

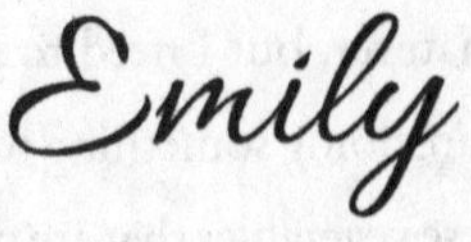

Emily

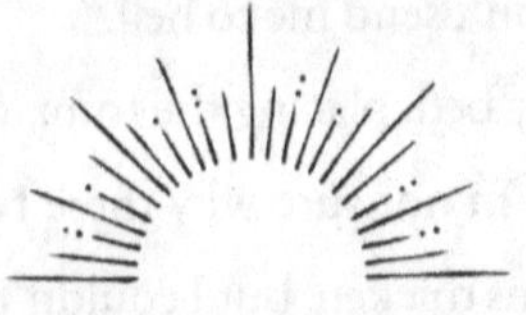

I close and lock the door behind me, leaning against it to catch my breath. I should have just gotten myself off nights ago when my mind wandered. It's been too long since I've touched myself—I can't even remember the last time. When I was with Darrell, I'd masturbate often. He never got me off, so the sex *with* him was just *for* him. The years of self-satisfaction led to more than proficient skills in taking care of myself in all ways. But ever since I made the plan to leave him and turn my life around, sex has been the last thing on my mind. I got a job at a parish, obviously, I wasn't planning to get fucked anytime soon.

I never imagined being boarded up with two of the world's hottest, most untouchable men. Mix my new living situation with the giant gap in my orgasm calendar—it's a recipe for disaster, or in my case, being turned on by fucking produce. I need this job. If I don't come, I fear I might lose my goddamn mind and completely offend everyone around me.

"Okay, God. I'm really sorry for what I'm about to do in your umm... house or whatever, but I need to get my head straight. These damn priests are doing something to me, and now there's something about these vegetables that are making me all hot and bothered. Please don't send me to hell."

I walk over to my bed, placing the tomato and cucumber on my bedside table. I'm not sure why these two vegetables make the blood in my veins thicken, but I couldn't bring myself to cut them up for tonight's salad. Something in me screamed to take them away from the kitchen. There were plenty of vegetables in the garden that I barely even noticed, but when I touched these two, it was like electricity shot through my nervous system. It's probably their texture. The cucumber is so hard and long with a slight curve. The tomato feels firm in my hand—its skin shiny and smooth. Couple these facts with my weird cucumber dick dream from the other night, and I think I've discovered my oddly specific perversion.

I rush back to my bedroom door, double-checking it's locked before I shimmy out of my blue jeans, kicking them out of my way. Gail is out of town for the next two weeks—visiting family, and although I didn't see them this morning, I'm scared shitless that the priests will walk in on me, although the thought does turn me on. Oh God, that's so inappropriate. I need to fix this urgent need. Now.

I walk back to my freshly made bed and lie on the comforter. I didn't bring a vibrator. That item didn't seem acceptable in a place like this, but it doesn't matter now because as I trail my fingers down my torso and under my black lacy underwear, I'm already soaking wet. Just the small touch of my fingertip on my swollen clit pulls a soft moan from my lips. My eyes nearly roll back to my head, imagining my dream. Father Robert standing before me—his dark eyes shadowed by his curly hair, his hold on my jaw as he wrestled with his belt buckle.

Father Laurent comes to mind. I don't recall my dream, but our conversation in the kitchen the other night. He was so close to me, the milk dripping down his chin and his hair a mess from a restless sleep. God, all I wanted was for him to pull my stool closer to his and wrap me in his arms. Of course, neither of these fantasies will ever happen, but here in my room, alone with my thoughts, anything is possible.

"Oh, Father," I moan. Imagine them both kissing up my neck, their hands splayed over my breasts, my abdomen, reaching down below my underwear like I'm doing to myself now. I don't increase the tempo of my single finger. The pent-up sexual frustration and the images dancing in my head are already too much.

I bite the palm of my hand, suppressing a cry. If the Fathers heard me, what would they think? The thought sends a shudder through my body even if my brain fights the urge to succumb to my desires—to remove my hand and see what happens. My hand falls to my side, and my head rolls to my shoulder. My eyes are still clamped shut, lost in my fantasy. Thankfully, I'm not drunk enough in my euphoria to make that stupid decision. I remain quiet, clamping my lips together.

My finger lazily rubbing my clit already feels too good. I just need to increase the tempo a tiny bit, and I'd reach that edge—clear my mind and let the wave of comfort roll over me. But something is missing. I'm empty. I need something to fill me.

My eyes shoot open, and the first things that catch my eye are the tomato and cucumber sitting on my side table. I whimper, immediately returning my palm to my mouth. It's like someone shot me up with a drug just from the sight of them. What is wrong with me, and why did I feel the need to bring them into my room?

I'll be ashamed of myself later. Now I need that tomato and cucumber—my desire taking over any rational thought. I reach for them, taking the cucumber in one hand and the tomato in the other. "God, I'm so sorry," I whisper, gazing at the produce before I succumb to the intrusive thought blaring through every corner of my mind.

9

Robert

I'm a tomato. A fucking tomato. Actually, I'm pretty sure I'm in some fucked up, spoiled wine-induced dream. When I opened my eyes this morning in the garden, Laurent lying beside me as a cucumber, I was pretty sure I died and ended up in the worst kind of hell, but now here I am in Emily's room. She pulls her shirt and bra up, revealing her perky and pebbled breasts. I'm a fucking tomato, but I'm pretty sure I'm in heaven, or more likely—the best and most fucked up dream my brain has ever conjured. This doesn't feel like a dream, though. As she rubs me down her skin, slowly moving me until she reaches the peak of her mound, I nearly pass out from the sensation. It feels so real.

It's been so long since a woman has touched me, or I've seen breasts, or felt hardened nipples under my fingertips. God, I used to love sucking on a woman's chest, flicking and biting until they were squirming under me, begging me to do more—to touch her cunt—to fuck her. The begging was my favorite. Now Emily whispers under the roll of my bulbous form, "Oh, God, yes, please." Her chest heaves rapidly, and she is barely able to control herself. It's all too much. Once I wake up, I'll be covered in my semen—I'm sure of it.

Emily grasps a cucumber in her other hand. It's Laurent. I have no fucking idea why I know that. It's not like he spoke to me or has any familiar facial features on his green and textured form. He looks like a regular fucking cucumber, but I know he's Laurent more than I know that I'm a tomato. No form could hide him from me. I'd recognize him even in the grave.

Emily drags Laurent across her skin, dipping between the valleys of her beautiful mountains where I'm perched in my bliss. He's so close to me. If only I could reach out and touch him, it would make this odd experience even more wonderful. He passes by, and I watch as she brings him down her abdomen. She tenses as she drags him over her cunt, pausing at her pelvic bone as if she needs to collect herself.

I want to cry out. The torture of not being able to react to the euphoria bubbling up inside intensifies. Will I explode if it becomes too much? I don't care. If my punishment from God for my thoughts is ending up a ketchupy mess across Emily's walls—I'll pay the price. It's all worth it as I watch Emily bring Laurent lower—to her entrance.

I want to be closer, to witness as Emily inserts Laurent into her warm and wet treasure. As if this is truly a gift from God instead of a curse, Emily lowers me, my skin slipping across the moisture rising from her pores. Her heat radiates from her core, beckoning me like a siren song. There's no room for shame. I'm a tomato, after all. This isn't real. The saintly rules don't apply here in this other universe where the three of us ended up.

I revel in the joy as I sit atop her cunt. She slowly presses me against her throbbing clit, using my hard mass to rub at her pleasure point. Her soft whimpers grow louder, and I try to apply more pressure or increase the speed at which she moves me. I want nothing more than to be a culprit in her delight, but I am at her will—unable to contribute except through my thoughts.

I nearly melt out of my skin once I see Laurent inserted into Emily. Her hand wraps around him, pushing him deep within her—only a small nub of his green bottom sticking out. It excites me that she can take him so readily. She's such a good girl, taking almost every inch of him. God, do I want to be inside of her. Laurent's a lucky bastard, but I can't complain. I have the best seat in the house—riding Emily's cunt, watching Laurent drown in Emily's pussy.

She's so quiet, muffling her moans, biting her lips to suppress her screams. God, do I want to hear the full extent of her arousal. Even as I feel her shake and the wetness allowing me to slide over her folds, it's not enough. Of course, fucking her as a tomato isn't enough. It will never be enough until I can take her fully and have her sobbing around my cock. But this is as good as it will ever get, whatever this thing is that's playing before me.

Of course, this is a dream or some sort of other reality. Emily wouldn't be fucking a cucumber or tomato. She's so beautiful with her doe eyes, plump lips, and the light freckles sprinkled across her nose. She could have whatever man she wanted. Granted, the only two men in her proximity are Laurent and me, and we aren't available for fucking—unless, of course, we're in a fucked up alternate reality as a cucumber and tomato.

In this fantasy, I can believe anything I want. My brain clings to the notion that Emily knows it's Laurent and me. She can sense us in the way I can feel Laurent. This most definitely is a blessing from God because right as this thought pops into my head, Emily cries out, "Father!" before biting her hand again to suppress her noises. Something bubbles in me, and my skin tightens as if something's about to burst from me.

I wonder if she can feel the glee taking control of me, becoming too much, because she increases her speed, rubbing me frantically against her clit as she thrusts Laurent in and out of her, the noise squelching around me. "Oh, Father," she moans as she comes under me, her body tensing as she sputters toward her edge. I've never felt an orgasm so acutely. Her vibrations shake me as her pussy accumulates more and more moisture. I want to drown in her, die right here atop her cunt.

It all becomes too much. There's a pop and wetness around me. I burst. A small hole opens at the bottom of me, and my literal seed drips onto Emily's skin. This can't be good. I just exploded, but it almost feels like release—like a strange version of tomato come. Warmth envelopes me until my vision blurs and my consciousness melts away. Maybe I am dying, but God, what a fucking way to go.

10

Emily

A crow caws in the distance, dragging me from my slumber like a rope pulling me from a hole. My eyes snap open, and it takes me a moment to remember where I am. It's almost dark. The light from my bedroom window is only a warm, orange flicker. I'm rested but could also fall asleep for another few hours. I can't remember the last time I napped that hard. Hours must have passed since I fell asleep earlier today. I'd almost forgotten how relaxing an orgasm could be. Damn, I guess I must make this a more regular thing. Maybe not with the produce, though. That was a little weird.

Besides, I didn't enjoy mutilating vegetables. I somehow made them burst and had to clean cucumber and tomato gunk from my crotch. Okay, maybe I actually liked cleaning that up and even tasted a little bit of it, as weird as that sounds, but I will need to head to the pharmacy at some point because I most definitely contracted a yeast infection.

I'm still lying on my back, not ready to move and finish all the tasks I didn't complete. *Shit.* I have a job to do. I wasn't hired to masturbate and sleep the day away. I sit up, attempting to grab the clock on the bedside table to catch the time, but my eyes never make it. They freeze on the two men curled up at the bottom of my bed.

I scream, kicking their unconscious bodies until they startle and topple off my too-small bed. It's not just two men. It's the priests. "What the fuck!" I yell, clutching my blanket to my chest to hide my pushed-up top. How did I not notice two six-foot men curled up at the bottom of my full-sized bed? Damn, that orgasm must have knocked me out.

Father Robert and Father Laurent rise to their knees on the floor, clutching their heads and looking around as if they are both as confused as I am. "What's going on?" Father Robert says, looking down at his body. He wears a white T-shirt and navy sleep pants. I track his gaze, noticing the wet spot at his crotch. Oh my god, this is mortifying. Is this God's punishment for fucking a cucumber? Surely, he wouldn't bring the priests into this. They didn't do anything wrong.

The thought of the produce has my head swiveling. It should be the least of my concerns right now, but I don't want the Fathers to catch the cucumber and tomato I smuggled into my room—sure, my perverted act would be too obvious.

"Man, did I just have the most fucked up dream," Father Laurent finally says, running his fingers through his mop of golden hair, looking a little more amused than Father Robert, or I imagine I look right now.

"What are you two doing in here?" I croak, my voice loud and strained.

Father Robert stares ahead at Laurent, befuddlement strewn upon his face, and I can't help but notice the fine whispers of stubble poking out on his jaw—further accentuating his image of being ill-prepared. "I have no idea." He shakes his head, stands to his feet, and covers his crotch with his giant hands. "I'm so sorry, Emily. I don't know how this happened, but we'll leave." His eyes slip momentarily to my chest, still covered by my blanket, before diverting to the floor. A small movement catches my attention from the other side of his hands. His cheeks blush. Oh my God, did I just give a priest a boner?

Father Laurent falls to his back, laughing. "Dude, what was in that wine? I had a dream I was a fucking cucumber!"

Father Robert catches my eyes, his expression wide.

"And Robert, you were a tomato! I'll keep the rest of it to myself, but holy shit, was it wild."

Robert turns to Laurent, his posture rigid. "What will you keep to yourself?"

Laurent remains on the floor, his hands over his eyes and a smirk still on his lips. "Believe me, you don't want to know."

Robert steps closer to him, seeming to grow taller. His voice is gruff and powerful. "What happened in your dream?"

Laurent sobers, sitting up and eyeing Robert. "Why?"

"Because I dreamed I was a tomato, and you were a cucumber."

There's no way. Are they playing some sort of cruel joke on me? Is this penance for masturbating in their home? I adjust myself, feeling uncomfortable, and the bed squeaks. The two priests whip their attention to me as if suddenly remembering I'm there.

"Maybe we should discuss this privately," Robert says, his eyes still on me as he extends a hand to Laurent on the floor, helping him to his feet.

I clear my throat. "I brought a cucumber and tomato into my room earlier today." Why did I admit that? There's no way what I'm thinking is true. It was just a cucumber and tomato, nothing more. Even if there seemed to be some supernatural attraction pulling me toward the produce, I was just super horny. That can be the only possible explanation. Maybe they were peeping in on me, saw what happened, and are teaching me a lesson. But maybe I don't care. Maybe I want to see just how these two will punish me.

Father Robert's eyes darken, and he steps toward me. Lost is the embarrassment coating him moments ago. In its place is a towering man set on finding answers. "Where are they?"

"Where is what?

"The cucumber and tomato."

"Oh, umm." I quickly pull down my shirt and drop the blanket, leaning forward to feel around. I left them in my bed after I cleaned myself up, but they're gone. Looking back up, I see that both of them have sat at the end of my bed, staring at me, their eyes tracking my every movement. I can't tell if they're mad or want to devour me.

I gulp. "I don't know. They're gone."

"What did you do with the cucumber and tomato, Emily? When you brought them into your room." Father Robert's legs hang off the bed. He leans forward, his veiny and muscular arms holding him up. I look at Laurent, suddenly feeling scared. His eyes are just as intense, but he smirks, his eyes flicking from Father Robert to me.

"Am I in trouble?" I can't hide the nerves around my words. My heart beats along with a warmness between my legs. I'm scared but also incredibly turned on. They're so close, so casual on the edge of my bed, and the way they're both looking at me—as if I'm in trouble, but they are so very pleased about it—it's taking over all my rational thoughts. The thoughts that this is wildly inappropriate and probably not at all what I'm imagining.

"Why would you be in trouble?" Robert asks, slowly leaning closer to me.

"Did you watch me? Is that what this is about?"

Laurent speaks up. "Watch you doing what?"

"Where did you put the tomato, Emily?" His hand is on my thigh, its weight removing all the air from my lungs. "Am I getting warmer?" His voice is so low, so heated. Laurent is at his side, placing another hand on my thigh.

"I don't know why I did that. I don't usually do that sort of thing with objects." I'm struggling to breathe, my eyes locked on Father Robert's, too scared to watch where he's moving.

He leans forward, his lips at my ear, and I feel the ghosts of his fingers between my thighs under the blankets. "I don't know why, but I think I was that tomato, Emily. You rubbed me on top of your swollen clit."

That snaps me out of it. I crane my neck away from his lips. "What are you talking about?"

Father Laurent leans in, his face next to Robert. "So it wasn't a dream. I really was the cucumber?"

I grab their shoulders, holding them both back. "What are you two talking about?" Did I stumble into some cult, or are these two just run-of-the-mill crazy? I'm beginning to realize why people fall into crazy ideologies. With leaders that look like these two, I'd drink the Kool-Aid.

Father Robert grabs my hand, still on his shoulders, his bicep flexing. He takes in a gulp of breath, and his eyes droop momentarily as if my touch disarmed him. He's taking back control. He breathes out, his eyes digging back into me. "You said you don't normally fuck objects."

I interject. "I did not say that."

"I know what you meant. I believe you."

"You believe what?"

"I believe you don't normally fuck objects."

I turn my attention to Laurent, raising my eyebrow. "So both priests have a dirty mouth?"

He shrugs with a smile. "Among other things."

Robert grabs my jaw and jerks my attention back to him. "If you don't normally shove cucumbers up your cunt or rub tomatoes over your tits, why the fuck did you do it today?"

"I... I... don't..."

He grips my jaw harder. "You know. Say it."

"I felt something. There was something different about that cucumber and tomato, something I can't explain." It's completely irrational what they're implying—impossible, but they're so convincing. His eyes, his grasp, his words, I'm drowning in them—reason leaving me.

Robert turns to Laurent, still holding my jaw. "What do you think?"

"I sure felt like a cucumber."

I pull back from Robert's touch, covering my mouth. "Oh, my God. I'm so sorry." I'm fully convinced at this point—at least for now.

They both snap their attention to me, their faces inches away from mine. "Why?" Laurent asks, as if my apology is the most confusing part of all of this.

"If all this is true, then what I did to you two was horrible."

Robert shrugs, turning to Laurent. "Well, I don't know if I would say that. I enjoyed myself."

"Me fucking too," Laurent says with a smile, eyes locked on Robert's.

"But you're both priests. Aren't you not supposed to have sex with women."

Laurent replies. "Ah, but we weren't priests when we were fucking you. I was a cucumber, and Robert was a tomato. Maybe this is from God. Maybe he wanted this to happen."

Something washes over Robert's face as if considering this. He stands abruptly. Gone is the abrasive man—controlling the room. In his place stands a puddle of nerves. "Well, we're not produce now. We need to leave. I'm sorry, Emily. This is completely inappropriate. Laurent, let's go." He turns before I can say more.

Everything's happening so fast. I don't know what to think, but I do know just moments before, Father Robert's lips were inches away from my own, his hand just a reach away from my pussy. "Wait! What's going on?" I look to Laurent, his expression as confused as I feel. He shrugs but stands, following after Robert.

Robert steps toward me but remains at the door. The veins in his neck bulge as he grabs Laurent's wrist. He points a finger at me. "I don't know if this is a test, blessing, or curse, but I do know that I'm not a tomato right now, and he's not a cucumber. I'm about two seconds away from losing my control and taking advantage of you. We need to separate and collect ourselves." He turns to Laurent. "We need to pray and ask God for guidance." Robert flings the door open and throws himself out, pulling Laurent behind him. Before Laurent disappears, he looks at me, rolling his eyes as if to apologize for his friend's irrational behavior.

The door shuts, and I'm alone. Alone, utterly confused, and completely turned on.

11

Robert

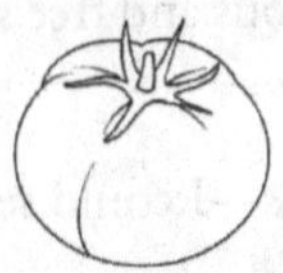

If only the world could pause for a day or two. If only I could spend my time alone in my room and contemplate the Earth-shattering events of the last twenty-four hours. But, unfortunately, I still have a job to do. My church needs me, and my to-do list with Gail out of town is longer than ever. I do thank God Gail wasn't here to walk in on our conversation yesterday evening. She doesn't live at the parish like we do, but she arrives to work early and leaves late. She most definitely would have caught a whiff of the events that transpired.

After leaving Emily's room, I created as much distance as possible from Laurent—locking my door and refusing to open it even when he knocked gingerly in the lonely hours of the night.

I've always known it wasn't as serious for Laurent as it was for me—the whole priest thing. Of course, we don't hide our crude language in front of each other, and we both have more progressive interpretations of the Bible, but he always takes his jokes and ideas a little further than I would. His shoulders don't sag with the weight of the responsibilities of the church, while my spine bends under the pressure. I'd always thought that was just his personality; living a life without hardships molded him into something more joyous and free spirit, but now I see how far he's willing to go.

He had no reservations—I could see it in his eyes. My cock begged to reach between Emily's legs—to show her just what I would do if I was in control and not a useless tomato. I could read her so well. Her whole expression swelled—her eyes, her lips, the way her chest pushed forward—she wanted me to touch her, to take her. And Laurent wouldn't have stopped me. He would have joined in, touching her in all the places I missed—maybe doing more. He was disappointed when I told him we needed to leave. I'm too weak. I can't carry both of our moralities, at least not in my current state.

I've spent all morning successfully avoiding him. Running around like a chicken without my head, acting like all the various administrative tasks Gail left for me were code red when, in reality, the latest order of communion bread could have been dropped off at the steps and the 501(c)(3) could have been sent to our tax person when she returned. I needed to get my thoughts together before I talked to him. He would just muddle things.

Now, it's time for my afternoon confessions. The confessional booth is a wooden structure about the size of two bathroom stalls. It has a partition with a small grille separating the penitent from the priest, so I'm unable to see who confesses, although I can usually tell by the voice. I never discuss what is confessed, not even with Laurent. Inside is a bench for the penitent and a chair for the priest on the opposite side. The booth is dimly lit, creating a solemn atmosphere. We keep the booth open for a few hours during the day. Lunchtime is most popular for the farmers, who take a midday break from the fields to get their hearts right with God. I'm eager for the space to myself and to hear the trivial transgressions of my community.

"Pray for the strength to overcome envy and to rejoice in the goodness that others experience. As penance, I ask that you pray for your neighbor's success and ask God to help you find contentment and peace in your own life," I respond after Mr. Harris confesses his jealousy over his neighbor's corn fields.

"Yes, Father," he replies before I hear the door to his side of the confessional booth open, and he shuffles out. If only my sins could be so simple. If only I could know if I actually sinned or not. Can produce sin?

I have a moment alone. I breathe out and rest my head against the wooden wall behind me. *God, give me a sign. What is happening, and what am I supposed to do about it?* I pray silently, hoping my tortured thoughts aren't bleeding through to my patrons.

The quiet moment doesn't last. The visitor door shuts on the other side, and the sounds of breath and shuffling come through the porous divider. "The Lord is merciful and ready to forgive you. Speak freely and know that His grace is abundant," I say, straightening my shoulders.

He doesn't even try to mask his voice. "Bless me, Father, for I have sinned. It has been ten years since my last confession."

I roll my eyes. "Fuck off, Laurent." I reach for the door, ready to escape the small booth that's already become too hot.

"Wait!" He sounds urgent and desperate, something I'm not used to. "Stop avoiding me. We need to talk about this. I'm as confused as you are."

I sigh and slump back against my seat, rubbing my palms against my face. "I don't know if I'm ready to talk about it with you."

"Who else can you talk to about this?"

"God."

"And what has he said?"

"Nothing yet."

He scoffs. "Figures."

"What are you implying?"

"Doesn't all of this make you question things?"

"You're a priest, Laurent. You've devoted your whole life to God. Is this all it takes to make you start questioning him?"

"All it takes? Robert, we turned into fucking produce and were fucked by our cook, and some supernatural sexual charge washed over us. This isn't a minor incident."

I scoff, shaking my head. "Who said there was a sexual charge? Speak for yourself."

His voice gets closer as if he's pressing himself against the divider. "Who are you lying to right now? Yourself? Because it sure as fuck isn't me. I saw the way you looked at her. You touched her, inches away from her cunt. Is that how you normally act around women?"

"No!" I yell, getting closer to the divider, my blood pressure rising in panic. "Okay, okay. Maybe there's something else to all of this besides being produce, but this doesn't disprove God for me. It must mean something. God works in mysterious ways."

It's silent for a moment. I imagine Laurent's satisfied that I'm admitting the truth. It does feel better to get part of my feelings off my chest. Of course, it's not the full truth. I can't come right out and say it—how the sexual charge isn't just a charge, it's a whole damn power plant, zipping through my body the moment Emily stepped onto the property. Maybe for a moment, when I was a tomato, I thought it was God's plan. Maybe he turned us into vegetables for us to get an ounce of sexual release, and then we'd be cured. We could return to our lives of celibacy, no longer driven by the flesh. It doesn't feel that way now. If anything, it's worse.

His voice is heavy—dreamlike. "It did feel holy, didn't it?"

I don't reply.

"It's been so long since I'd been inside a woman." He gives a soft, pained chuckle. "It wasn't in the way I was used to, but

Jesus Christ, did it feel good. I didn't realize how much I'd missed the feeling."

My eyes shut, and my head lulls back. "Yeah," is all I manage to say.

"It was also torture, though, not being able to touch her back. Maybe that's our penance."

"Hell of a penance." I smile.

"Yeah. I never thought I'd dream of being a cucumber again."

I sit in the silence for a moment, registering no sign of life near the confession booth. I gather the nerve to ask my question, the tension around us from earlier melting away. "What did it feel like? Being inside of her?"

"It felt like my whole body was my cock."

"Really?"

"Maybe it's just because I haven't been laid in a while, but it was the best sex I ever had."

"When's the last time?"

"I'd been laid?"

"Yeah."

He thinks for a minute. "Probably the day before seminary school?"

"The day?!"

I can hear his shoulders rise in a shrug. "I wanted to make sure I got it out of my system." I chuckle. I try to think back to the last time I'd had sex. I can't remember. It was probably during a bender, a drunk night with a girl I never saw again. Sex had never been anything but just a pastime—fine in the moment but completely forgettable. That's why I figured it would be so easy for me to become a priest. These feelings are uncharted waters.

Laurent clears his voice. "Father, I must confess a sin."

I roll my head to the side. "Oh, cut it out."

"I jerk off. As much as possible," he says quickly.

Images run through my head—the look on his shadowed profile from across our dorm, his hands underneath his blanket. My breath heavies in my chest. "I've jerked off, too," I concede.

His breath grows louder. "Really? I thought you stopped when we got our own rooms."

There it is. The thing we've never talked about. "Why did you think that?" I grip my thigh, my slacks tenting.

"I don't hear you."

I palm my cock. I'm drunk on the tension now, my brain twisting to images—my mouth not connected to the rest of me. "Do you try? To hear me?"

A soft whimper seeps through the holes between us. "Every night, I listen for your moans. I still remember the way you sound." His belt buckle jingles. His clothes rustle.

"I'm much quieter now." I reach down my pants, pulling myself out slowly.

He tsks. "Such a shame. You have such a pretty moan."

I groan, stroking myself. Precum dollops at my head, and I lather my length, moving slowly, afraid noise will pierce this moment.

"Father, I have another confession."

I don't reply.

"I'm touching myself right now."

I moan.

"Yes, Father. There it is. Just like I remember. Soft and sweet."

His words are like gentle hands around me. I keep my eyes closed, imagining his soft lips around my cock.

"Are you touching yourself, Father?" His voice is pained, as if holding himself back. His strokes are noisier. He's moving fast up and down his slick cock. I remember his noises well. I'm brought back to that night when it was just the two of us, lost in our bodies, but now the space is even closer. I can almost feel his warmth through the thin particleboard between us.

"Yes," I reply, my body melting into a puddle of warm butter. I'm not a priest right now. I'm not even human—just nerve endings, just pleasure.

"Are you thinking of me, Father? Are you thinking of me, stroking my cock on the other side of this wall? Imagining your mouth around my cock?"

His words are dirty, sinful, and shameful, but my body responds outside my reason. It's like his words are a nail, prying open the dam of my control. I moan, messy, loud, and desperate. Warmth erupts from my shaft, covering my hand as I use it to squeeze out every last drop in me.

Laurent cries out next to me, just as deep and desperate. We breathe in unison as the fog clears. The quietness loudens, and it's like someone ripped the roof off, letting in the harsh sun. I look down at my mess, my placid dick covered in the evidence of my sin. I panic, shoving myself back into my pants. I don't say a word as I stumble out of the booth, retreating back to my room as fast as I can.

12

Emily

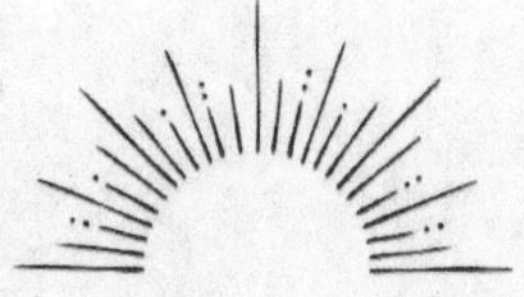

The wind whips across my cheeks, sending my brown hair over my eyes and making me pause from my work to adjust myself. Dirt covers my hands, and ripe and juicy vegetables fill my woven basket—everything in the garden except tomatoes and cucumbers. I stayed far away from those lines of produce.

It's been nice to spend the entire day busy, getting my hands dirty. My back hurts from bending over, and sweat coats my upper lip. Now that the wind stopped me from my obsessive need to move, interrupting me and forcing me to still for a moment, my brain rushes with the mess of what happened. Stupid wind.

I breathe out, unable to stay mad at my environment for long. It's just so beautiful. It's like I'm smack dab in the middle of a postcard. Rows of lush greenery trail over hills, skies dotted with white clouds, and farm animals making noises in the distance.

It's all too good, making me feel unworthy of this life. I know I don't deserve it, but I don't care. I'm not giving it up. This is my home now.

I stand, wiping my hands on my jeans and straining to pull the basket over my shoulder before walking back toward the parish. The sun lowers over the hills, making the sky warm and golden. It's almost time for me to start preparing dinner. I've spent all day out in the fields, avoiding the priests. I woke early, quickly made muffins for their breakfast, and wrote a note about sandwiches in the fridge before hiding out for the day. I needed distance from the two.

Right now is the first time all day that I've pondered what happened. They told me they turned into a tomato and cucumber. Two days ago, I didn't know if I believed in God, and now they want me to believe they transformed into vegetables. I'd be crazy to believe them, but I guess I am crazy because even if they didn't tell me they were the cucumber and tomato I got off with, I'd know something wasn't normal about that produce.

I've done some weird shit throughout my life but never have I stuck a cucumber up my vagina or rubbed a tomato over my clit. I'd never do something like that unless supernatural forces were at play. Besides, why would they lie to me? At first, I thought it might be a ruse to get me to confess to masturbating in the Lord's house, but then they admitted to enjoying it. Both of their hands were on my thigh, and they looked like they wanted to bend me over and fuck me from both ends. Father Robert looked mortified once he noticed what he was about to do, running out of my room with an erect cock stuffed between his legs. They fully believe they were the tomato and cucumber and have no reason to lie to me. I believe them, even if my years of hard-earned reason beg me to reconsider.

The real question is, why did this happen, and will it happen again? Will I turn into a zucchini or something? The thought sends terror down my spine as I enter the kitchen, swinging the basket on the counter. But then I think about the priests using my zucchini body to please them, and my fear wash away. Maybe it wouldn't be so bad.

I open the refrigerator, pull out the steaks I've been marinating all day, and place them on the counter to come to room temperature before cooking them on the cast iron. I hear the priests rustling in their rooms down the hall, making my palms clammy. A part of me hoped they would skip dinner so we wouldn't need to discuss what happened. But another part of me knows this will be the best time. Gail will be home from vacation soon, and there's no way I want to bring another person into this mess.

My mind wanders as I prepare roasted potatoes and broccoli and mix up a demi glaze for the steak. I need to be careful. Priests are not supposed to have sex with women. Men love to blame women for their fuckups. I don't think Father Robert and Father Laurent are bad guys, but you never know with men. They could use my job against me and threaten me if anything leaks. They don't have to worry about me telling anyone, though. I have no one to tell, and who the fuck would even believe me?

As I plate the steaks and vegetables and place them on the big oak table on the other side of the kitchen, I realize all this time in my head is only making things worse. I need to talk to them and clear the air, or I will give myself an aneurysm. I set down a plate for myself and sit at the head of the table. "Dinners ready!" I call, just as the last rays of sun slip through the window.

A few seconds later, two doors creak open almost simultaneously, and footsteps shuffle down the hall. I hold my breath, only releasing it once Father Laurent appears, his eyes twinkling mischievously as they grab hold of mine. Father Robert follows after, his eyes underlined by dark bags and his attention nervously darting away from mine. They sit at their plates on either side of me, quiet except for their chairs scraping against the hardwood floor.

I give them a second, allowing them to enjoy their first bites of food before folding my hands in front of me and clearing my throat. "We need to talk."

Father Robert's spine stiffens, and he doesn't look away from his plate. Laurent smiles, pushing away his plate and lounging back in his chair, holding the back of his head in a relaxed position, revealing his muscular underarms. "Okay, what should we talk about?"

Father Robert slams his utensils against the table, glaring up at Laurent.

I cut through the tension. "Let's not play games. Obviously, what happened yesterday was insane. Do either of you have any idea why it happened? Is this a God thing?"

Father Robert pushes his food around with his fork. "Nothing in the Bible suggests this has happened before, but it could still be a God thing."

Father Laurent chuckles. "Yeah, especially the sex part. That felt very godly."

My cheeks heat, and I'm momentarily thrown off kilter.

Robert doesn't seem fazed by the comment, as if too focused on the inner workings of his thoughts. His eyes grow wide as if an idea formed. "That old woman was saying all that weird stuff the other day."

"What old woman?" I ask, my brain refocusing.

Laurent sighs. "This batty old woman I've never seen before cornered us after Robert's sermon the other day. She was just rambling."

"The Harvest Moon, where spirits come to play. All that is hidden will be brought to light. It's up to you both to define the true fruits of your soul." Robert says, his expression haunting.

"You remember all that?" Laurent asks.

"What the fuck?" I yell before covering my mouth. The priests give me a wide-eyed look. Right, they are cool priests. They curse and want to fuck me. I can curse in front of them. I drop my hands. "Why are you just now mentioning this? She obviously knew something like this would happen."

Laurent waves his hand in dismissal. "She was off her meds."

I stare at him, dumbfounded.

Robert clears his throat. "She's right. It wasn't a coincidence. We turned into fucking vegetables right after that creepy woman told us that."

"So what? We've got a witch on the loose? We're cursed? Aren't priests supposed to be immune to that?" Laurent says.

"Unless she's an angel," says Robert.

That shuts us all up.

I'm annoyed the priests haven't thought about the woman sooner. I'm unsure what the cryptic message means, but it obviously concerns what's happening. Even with this revelation, it doesn't explain why or what is going on. We can only hope that the woman returns and can explain things, whether she's a witch or an angel. I have a creeping suspicion that's unlikely. This feels like something we have to figure out on our own. I don't know why I'm lumped into this mess. I didn't get transformed into a vegetable, but I guess fucking the priests as produce now makes me an accomplice. "Has it happened again since yesterday?"

Robert shakes his head, finally bringing his eyes to mine. "No." Goosebumps pepper my skin. His gaze is shy—almost apologetic, but immediately sparks a heated response for me.

"Maybe it won't happen again then." I shrug, moving my gaze to my plate.

Father Robert nods in agreement, looking up at Laurent's bemused expression. Father Laurent chuckles. "Ah, don't be so pessimistic, you two. I'm sure God will let us have some fun soon."

Robert tenses, his grip tightening around his fork. "Laurent," he seethes, but a loud pop sounds through the room before he can finish his sentiment. I blink, and the priests have disappeared.

I scream, jumping to my feet. The priests haven't disappeared, though. A tomato and a cucumber take their place on their seats. I look down, assessing if I've also transformed. My body appears the same, except for the insatiable buzzing in the pit of my stomach. I run over and grab them in both hands, looking around to see if anything in the room changed. Maybe a witch hides in the corner, but it's just me. Alone with two of the sexiest vegetables in the world.

13

Laurent

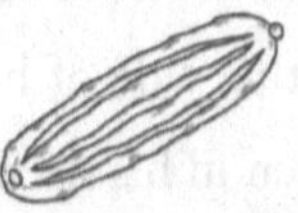

A rooster bellowing off in the distance drags me from my slumber, fanning my eyes open to allow in the early morning rays. I rub my head as I sit up. My neck hurts like a bitch from lying on the hardwood floor. I'm still in Emily's room at the side of her bed. I stand, gazing down at Emily curled up in the blankets, her arms thrown overhead and her brown hair a halo around her angelic face. I clench my hands, fighting them to resist reaching out and pressing a fingertip to her plush lips.

Last night, after we transformed, Emily picked us up, nervous and fidgety as she scanned the kitchen. She said nothing, but I could see the wheels in her head working. She didn't know what to do with us, and her body was a tingly mess. I imagine as much as mine was. To my joy, she brought us into her room, but my happiness quickly diminished when she placed us on the floor instead of bringing us into the bed with her.

She slept as poorly as I did, tossing and turning and her hands gripping her sheets. If only she'd allow her urges to take hold—to touch herself at the thought of us lying on her floor, to let loose like she did the day before. But now that she knows were sentient vegetables, she's shy. Such a shame.

Robert lies on the other side of her bed. He looks like he has a stick up his ass, even in his sleep. His brow furrows, and his hands ball into fists. I still love the asshole, even if he ruins all my fun. Who am I kidding? I love him even more for his stubbornness. It just makes me want to break him. I shiver at the thought of our moments together in the confessional booth yesterday. I've never felt closer to God. Finally, after all these years, I seeped into his hard exterior. I must thank Emily and the magical vegetable spell. It's awakening something in all of us.

I shift my weight to my other foot, making the floorboard creak. Emily's eyes dart open. I smile at her. "Hi," I whisper, sitting at the side of her bed. She recoils, sitting up and holding her blanket over her chest. God, I hate that I make her so nervous. I don't understand why. I'd bring her nothing but elation if she'd only allow it. "Good morning," I try again.

She squints at me, keeping her voice low, "You seem awful chipper after turning into a vegetable."

I shrug. "Maybe it's fun to be something different for a while. Besides, I woke up in a beautiful woman's bedroom. I've had worse mornings."

Her breath shudders, and she drops her blanket from her chest, revealing her hardened nipples pressed against her thin sleep shirt. "Are you flirting with me, Father?"

"Poorly, if you have to question." I crawl closer, looming over her body.

She smiles, the first time I've seen the beautiful curve since our late-night chat in the kitchen. She turns to Robert, still fast asleep on the floor beside us. "You two are so different."

I nod. "We're different vegetables, after all."

She laughs quietly. "Not just that. He is so serious about all of this while you seem to be having fun."

I nod. "It's one of my favorite things about him—his seriousness. It makes me want to join in on everything he cares about. Hell, it's why I'm a priest." She studies me momentarily, something like understanding shining in her brown eyes.

Robert grumbles from next to us, shooting up in alarm. "What happened?"

"Big orgy. Filled with carrots and celery. Just missed it."

Emily clucks and slaps my arm. "You both turned into vegetables again, and I brought you here. I was afraid something might happen to you out in the open. Even with no one else here, I couldn't risk it. Don't worry. I was a good girl and kept my hands to myself all night."

Such a good girl.

Robert stands, dusting himself off. "Yes, thank you. I was conscious, but I must have fallen asleep."

"What happens if you two turn into vegetables when you're giving a sermon or something?"

To my surprise, Robert clears his throat and sits on the edge of the bed. "It's only happened twice, once when we were alone with you, and maybe the first time, when we were in the field, we didn't turn into vegetables until you were nearby."

"I've been alone with Laurent before, and he didn't turn into a cucumber," Emily says.

I study Robert's side profile as he tightens around his bones. "You two were alone?"

She rushes. "Yes, but only for a late-night snack the first night I was here."

He whips his gaze to me, his jaw tense. I shrug. "Stayed human the whole time, but that was before the witch cursed us or whatever."

"True, or maybe it's only when you're alone with both of us."

"How can we be sure? Should I be following you both around?"

Robert sighs. "No. I don't think so. Of course, nothing is certain. None of this makes sense, but we can only hope that it won't happen more randomly."

I grab her hand. "I disagree. I definitely think you should follow me around. I feel rather cucumbery whenever I step into the shower."

Emily shakes her head and turns to Robert. "Is he always like this?"

"Usually only with me. I thought I trained him enough to be a gentleman in front of others." He pats my cheek, and I scrunch my face.

"I guess I'm special then," Emily says.

Robert connects his eyes with her. "Oh, you're definitely special." I could cut the tension between them with a spoon. I don't move—don't breathe, wanting it to last forever. Emily shakes herself, ridding the room of the moment. "So what now?"

"I've been thinking." Robert's cheeks blush, and he brings a leg onto the bed, making himself more comfortable.

"Oh, I love it when you think." I lean in, my heart racing.

"I've been a good priest."

"So good."

"I've never crossed the line. Always keep my thoughts pure."

"Unfortunately."

He throws me a look, and I clamp my lips.

He returns his attention to Emily. "My point is, this thing between the three of us," he motions. "It's stronger than anything I've ever felt. It almost feels like the pull I felt from God when I joined seminary school. Maybe this is a gift. I'm not sure why he chose to turn us into vegetables, but if I'm a tomato, I'm not a man of God. I'm just a veggie, and veggies can't sin."

My dick hardens, and I cross my legs, not wanting to jump the gun on what Robert is explaining. Emily's eyes are wide, and her shoulders are straight as she watches Robert's lips.

"Of course, I don't want to suggest anything you're uncomfortable with, but it seems you are attracted to us. As vegetables, I mean. I only offer to use us as you wish when we take that form." He turns to me. "I don't mean to speak for you. Please suggest…"

"Please, please speak for me." I turn to Emily, grabbing her hands. "I beg you to use my cucumber-self anytime you see fit." Her expression remains rigid, and I drop her hand. I thought she was waiting for Robert's acceptance, much like I was, but maybe my own eagerness was clouding my judgment. What was I thinking? She's a beautiful woman. Surely, she doesn't want to be part of our perverted manifestations. Even if she did use our bodies to please herself yesterday, that could have been a flux, a misjudgment.

"Okay," she finally says, her breath heavy.

"Okay," I repeat.

"But," she interjects.

"Oh no buts," I say.

"What if you two don't turn into vegetables again? It's only happened twice. Maybe that was it."

I turn my attention to Robert, leaning forward, his arms holding himself up, inches away from Emily. I know she's asking him. He's the holder of all of our fates. He's the boss, the owner of morality. If it was up to me, I'd say fuck it. Pin her to the bed and fuck her mouth while Robert took care of her cunt. And while I was at it, I'd finally grab Robert's cock, stroking it until he cried tears of joy. But it's not up to me. It never is. Not with Robert, at least.

"Then nothing happens. Then this was just a test from God to see if we would resist temptation, and we passed. We'll carry on as if nothing happened."

It's like someone stuck a needle into our lustful cocoon, and all the air zips out of the room. I hoped this would be more for Robert. More than just a mission for God. I hoped he would see what's between us—the feelings so strong that it's sucking in another person in our orbit.

"Okay," Emily replies.

My heart races as I study both of their faces. The tension is thick in the room. Here we are, alone together. When will it happen next?

After a few moments of silence, Robert grows uncomfortable, examining his watch. All of this is odd, but watching him look at the instrument on his wrist makes me realize that whenever we shift, everything on our body disappears, and whenever we shift back, it appears where it belongs. I can't believe I didn't think of it sooner. Who makes the rules in these sex-vegetable morphing realities? I guess I can't get hung up on the details. I'd go crazy.

"Well, I have a busy day ahead of me. I guess we'll just carry on and see what happens." Robert stands, eyeing us over before heading to Emily's door. When I don't follow, he stops and looks at me, clearing his throat.

"Fine," I whine, but as I stand, my ears pop. I blink, the room grows, and I'm lying on the floor, immobilized. I've never been so happy to be so helpless.

Emily gasps from above me, leaning over her bed and picking me up from the floor. She jumps to her feet, rushing to the spot Robert was moments before. In his place rests a juicy, red tomato. Emily picks him up and brings us both to her line of vision. "I guess this is happening now," she whispers. She stares at us for a moment, wetting her lips as if she's about to take a bite.

Please, for the love of God, bite me. Jesus Christ, does being a cucumber turn me into a masochist.

Her breath heavies and her eyelids droop just from the sight of us in her hands. "Oh my God," she moans. "Why does just looking at you two make me so fucking horny? This is so fucked up." She groans, throwing her head back in a pout before stomping to bed.

She lies flat on her back, placing us to the side of her before yanking down her silk sleep pants and pulling the matching cami over her head. She moves quickly as if annoyed and wants this to be done. I want to bend her over my knee and spank her. Doesn't she know that this is the only sexual reprieve I get except for taking myself in my hand? And even with that, I apparently risk the fiery pits of hell. This is holy—sacred. Robert said so, and whatever Robert says, I'll sow into every fiber of my beliefs.

She's naked, not a stitch of clothing on her. I wish she'd run me up and down every inch of her body, let me revel in the feel of her, but she's too shy now that she knows it's us. I understand. We can't encourage her—tell her how *good* she's being, how perfectly her cunt cries for us. It must feel vulnerable to perform with no support—to be the curator of this sexual experience for all of us. God, do I want to praise her, tie her up on the altar, and worship every inch of her skin. But this will have to do for now. It's more than enough for me.

Emily wraps her fingers around me again. A shiver runs through my body when she touches my green flesh. She brings me to her line of vision, studying me curiously. "I felt something," she whispers in disbelief. Can it be possible? Could I have willed myself to move?

I try again, exerting all my focus on making my body shake. I vibrate against her hand. "Oh, my god." She gasps. Her breath hitches, and she worms her legs around the other.

Robert must sense what I've just been able to do because she grabs him in her other hand and says, "You can vibrate, too? Sorry, boys. This isn't going to last long." She should know we're in control of this movement. We want her to come hard and fast. Finally, something to make me feel less helpless in all of this—something to contribute to this holy moment.

Emily lowers us to her breasts, rubbing us over her hardened nipples. "Fuck!" She cries as I will my vibrations to increase, the feel of her pebbled flesh against me eliciting more and more life from me. She drags me down her body, in between her breasts, over her stomach, and stops at her pelvic bone. She keeps Robert at her nipple as she lowers me, hovering me over her clit.

Her juices seep through my hardened skin. She's so wet, so sweet. I slide through her perfect cunt as easily as a fish swims through water. I push myself closer to her entrance, my home, the place where my body belongs. She doesn't fight my slight movements, allowing me to insert my tip. I want to do more—to pound into her until her walls clench around me. Maybe next time. Maybe I'll become more powerful every time we perform this sacred act. But right now, all I can do is vibrate as she slowly inserts me deeper and deeper.

She's so tight. Every inch of my skin tingles, making my vibrations increase. She cries out as the molten lava doubles throughout me. She brings Robert closer to me, and for a moment, our skin bumps against each other. I know what he feels. If it's anything like the elation rolling through me, it's too much, and now our skin touches. I might pass out. I don't know if I can take it anymore.

Emily brings Robert away, just above me, to her engorged clit. She's so close. I can feel it. I want it to last longer, but it's already too much. "Jesus Christ!" she cries as she increases her thrusts on me, her fingernails piercing me slightly.

The arousal builds to a dangerous level. I'm going to explode like last time, leaking my cucumbery seed inside Emily's cunt. Yesterday, I thought I died when my seed escaped me. I thought I was crushed as the relief washed over me, and I faded into darkness. Now I know what to expect. I'm about to bust like a can of biscuits, and it will be the best feeling I've ever felt.

Emily sobs, her walls closing in on me. The building inside me reaches its boiling point, and I burst—coating her walls. She could crush me with her tightness. I'm still firm and hard as her orgasms ripple in waves, but she's tight—the space growing smaller as if to juice me. No fear surrounds me. I'd love to die inside of her. If only Robert could join me. Both of us, encased by her, joined in nirvana and death.

A thought dawns on me through the fog. I'm willing to die with Robert here because I know I'll never live a life with him or with anyone. I already feel deeply for Emily—a dangerous thing since I'm not allowed to attach to anyone. I would rather be a cucumber than a human because I am more myself than ever before.

All my dreams are coming true, but maybe my dreams deserve more than this cucumber form.

14

Robert

Has God ever crafted a more beautiful day than today? It's like a fog had been following and has finally cleared. Flowers bloom brightly. Birds chirp sweetly, and my body feels sugary sweet in my skin. As I walk to the chapel to watch Laurent deliver a sermon to the congregation, a cool breeze tickles my skin, and God settles himself around me. I was right. God is the one who turned us into vegetables. He did it for us to experience and give pleasure, to be connected to another person. Everything's coming together. This is my destiny.

I passed out after squirting my seed over Emily's cunt and awoke to my human self in her bed. They were both asleep but rose from their slumber as I stirred. They couldn't mask their meek grins as much as I couldn't hide mine. "You both vibrated," Emily said, a hue warming her cheek.

"Maybe we become more powerful after every..." I wracked my brain for an appropriate title for what we just did. It wasn't sex. This was a sacred act from God. My mind settled on a word. "Session." I immediately regretted my choice. I made it sound clinical.

"Maybe." Emily nodded. She looked down, and her eyes grew wide as if she had just realized she was still naked.

I stood and turned to give her some privacy. After what had just happened, it was an odd gesture, but we were priests again, not vegetables.

Laurent followed suit. He hadn't spoken yet, which was unlike him. He was always making jokes, and what I had just said felt like the perfect set-up for one of his punchlines.

"How was it for you?" I asked as I looked over my shoulder at the back of Laurent's moppy head. "Are you okay?"

He glanced at me, snagging my eyes with his for just a moment before returning his gaze to the floor. "I'm fine. Great, even."

I cleared my throat. "Alright, well, I should be on my way. I've got sermons to prepare."

"Yeah, me too," Laurent said, following me as I walked to Emily's door.

"Okay. Well bye then." Emily said from her bed, now fully dressed. Before I slipped out, I caught my eyes with hers. Her cheeks were red, her hair a disheveled mess—beautiful as always, maybe even more so. Was it possible that she was becoming more stunning by the second? Maybe that was a blessing from God, too. I felt guilty for leaving her in such a rush. She deserved to be cuddled and whispered sweet nothings, but God had a higher calling for us all.

I'm about one hundred feet from the backdoor to the chapel, but my mind replays the events of the night before. From my front row seat atop Emily's mound, I marveled as her face contorted around her pleasure, her eyes half-lidded, her mouth parted just enough to release her soft moans. She was an angel sent from heaven and I would worship her body any chance I could, even if that only happened as a tomato.

I enjoyed every minute of being used for her pleasure, but unholy thoughts still danced in my head. I wanted to be in control—to hold her down, tell her what to do, and push her toward the edge until she was begging for release. She wanted it. I could see it in the way her eyes searched me. But both of our wants would have to go unsatisfied. We must be thankful for the blessing we received.

My attention snaps back to the moment as my hand reaches the doorknob of the chapel. I push down my cock in my slacks and replace the carnal images in my head with ones of the church. The body of Christ, the blood of Christ. *Fuck*. Now all I can think of is Emily's naked body strung up at the front of the sanctuary, me on my knees worshiping her as I drink from her cunt. This isn't helping. I groan before pushing the door open, praying that I can keep my brain and cock in check for the next hour.

It appears I'm not the only one with a scattered mind today. As I sit at the side of the pulpit, watching Laurent stumble through an ill-prepared sermon, I thank the Lord I'm not the one in his place. If anything, I thought he'd be giddy—more at ease, but he's a mess. His white collar hangs out from one side of his black shirt. His top button is undone. His hair is even more unruly than usual, and he nearly dropped the f-bomb after forgetting his train of thought and skimmed through his crumpled notes.

I clench the armrests of my chair and will my expression to remain neutral. If the congregation sees me rattled, it will make Laurent's fuck-up more obvious. Even though he's making that abundantly clear on his own.

Laurent is always relaxed—carefree. This is not good. He isn't taking our arrangement well. I should have known. After what happened in the confessional booth the other night, I should have seen that this was more for him. Yeah, I've thought about Laurent in that way, dreamed of pushing the boundaries with him, and reveled in the small moments we were alone together, but that's normal. A symptom of a life of celibacy. Right? He wants more. He always wants more.

Moments ago, I was positive this was a blessing from God, but now I'm not sure. I watch as Laurent drops his notes off the podium and mutters profanities under his breath. Can it be God's will if it's not positively affecting everyone involved? We need to talk.

By the grace of God, his sermon ends with, "Sorry for the mess-ups. It's like that one time I got my lips stuck in a gate." He chuckles awkwardly, shaking his head. "May the peace of the Lord be always with you."

What the fuck? Lips stuck in a gate? Why is he talking about his lips?

I stand, smiling at the patrons before stepping toward Laurent and grabbing his forearm. "What is wrong with you?" I whisper through gritted teeth.

Laurent pulls his arm back and narrows his eyes, his voice low, "It was a bad day. Cut me a fucking break."

"Gentleman?" A voice turns our attention away from one another and toward the tall man in a black shirt with a white collar at his neck. His brown curly hair makes him a head taller than Laurent.

Fuck. It's Bishop Archibald—our boss. He oversees all the regional churches, ensuring we're doing our job. Usually, his visits are scheduled. Maybe it's because of Gail's absence, but I did not expect him. How could I miss this man sitting in the audience? I must have been so distracted by Laurent's trainwreck of a sermon.

I shake the shock off my face, walking toward the stairs on the right side of the stage. "Bishop! What a pleasure to see you here today," I say as I approach, outstretching my hand.

He examines my offering over his small circular glasses, taking a deep breath before returning his attention to my face, not moving his hand to meet mine. "Yes, I had a free space in my schedule and decided to pay you two a surprise visit."

"What a pleasure!" Laurent says, his usual boyish smile returning to his face. He lowers his body and hops off the stage next to us. I grit my teeth at his casualness.

Bishop Archibald gives an unamused smirk, shaking his head at the two of us. Archibald has always been a hard ass, critiquing us over our sermons running short or a wrinkle in our robes. We're both usually on it. If there's one thing Laurent and I excel in the whole priestly domain, we can command a crowd and give a kick-ass sermon. Today did not reflect our abilities. It was Laurent up at the pulpit, not me, but we're seen as a team.

"May I have a private word with you both in your office?" He turns on his heel, not waiting for our response, and walks toward the back of the chapel.

Laurent and I give each other a wide-eyed look. Laurent says, "Maybe he'll turn into an asparagus before he can fire us."

I groan and roll my eyes, leaving Laurent's side and following after the Bishop. He's ridiculous, but maybe all priests do turn into produce in our parish now. If that's the case, I hope Emily doesn't find him. I don't want her fucking any other vegetables beside us. It's already complicated enough.

15

Laurent

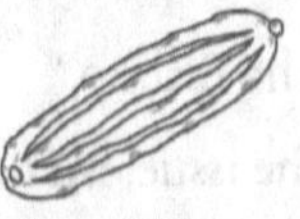

"**W**ell, we're not fired," I say, my voice rising an octave as Robert turns from shutting his office door after Bishop Archibald. "And he didn't turn into a vegetable, so we don't have to worry about that."

Robert's shoulders are tense, and he rolls his sleeves to his elbow as he walks to his desk. He balls his fists, accentuating the veins on his forearms, and he refuses to meet his intense gaze to mine. "We're not fired for now. You heard him. He suggested we take time off. Next time, it won't be a suggestion. How could you let this happen, Laurent?" He shuffles through papers on his desk, shaking his brown curly locks.

Anger boils in my blood, an uncommon feeling for me, at least with Robert. I lean over his desk, smacking down the papers in his hand. "Cut the shit. It's not like I'm the only one to experience a bad day at the pulpit. You've had your fair share of fuckups."

He stands, glaring at me. Even though he's two inches shorter than me, he's always been more intense, more frightening. It's one of the things I love about him. "Having a bad day is different than nearly saying fuck to a room full of widows and farmers. We behave the way we do in private but never in front of the congregation, let alone the Bishop."

"Well, maybe that's the issue, isn't it? Maybe what we do in private can't just stay there forever. Maybe our true selves will shine through one of these days."

His pupils expand, and his sneer fades. "What are you talking about?"

I stand straight, meeting him on the other side of his desk. "You know damn well what I'm talking about. What if this isn't enough for me, for all of us? What if I can't just whisper my profanities, live off your accidental brushes, or fuck a woman I'm growing to care for only as a cucumber. What if I want more?"

He shakes his head, anger returning to his dark eyes. He steps toward me, his finger pointed at my chest as I back away from his furry. "How could you be so selfish? This is bigger than all of us. This is God. You've taken a vow. I've obviously made a mistake. It wasn't the right choice to succumb to our urges as vegetables. That old woman must have been one of Satan's minions instead of an angel." He steps back. "We're done. No more fucking around as vegetables."

My stomach hollows. I was so determined moments before—certain that living at the edge of my desires wouldn't be enough, but now that Robert rips everything away from me in an instant, I'm back to my desperate self. What am I going to do? Leave the church? Would I truly be happier without Robert and now Emily? "Wait. No, you can't take that away from us. You said it was God."

"I was wrong. God obviously sent Bishop Archibald as a warning that we were on the wrong path."

"Robert, please." My voice shakes, and I grab his wrist. He looks down at where our skin meets. His expression softens a miniscule. "I've waited. I've been good. I've done everything you asked. I joined the seminary because I was looking for something more, something to follow. I think you both know it wasn't God for me. It was something else. I know you are devoted. This is it for you. I've always respected that. In fact, I admired you for it. But we finally have something. Something to fulfill our needs. Please don't take that away from me. I'm sorry I shouldn't have asked for more."

He scoffs but gets closer. My back hits the wall. "Do you think you're the only tortured soul to exist? You think I don't have urges that run my thoughts? You haven't been good. You haven't been respectful. Every breath you take tempts me. Every movement you make brings me closer to the edge of my breaking point. I've always barely held on by a thread. And then this miracle or curse, or whatever it is, happened, and I thought maybe it was a gift from God for resisting you for all these years.

But it's obviously too much for us. I don't want to be without you, Laurent." He slams a fist against the wall at the side of my head. "Fuck! This could be the end of us if we let it."

My heart hammers in my chest. His breath tickles my lips. Tears rest in the corner of his eyes. I hear his words. I feel his pain, but he doesn't realize what he's saying. Everything I felt over the years rests on his lips. He's too wound up in God that he doesn't realize what he's admitting. A force comes over me. Maybe it's God. Maybe it's something bigger, but I can't resist. I lean in, crashing my lips against him.

I'm an idiot. This isn't what he wants, but I can't help myself. I expect him to pull away and punch me in the jaw, but he surprises me. His lips part, and he melts into me. My dick hardens, pressing against my slacks. I push into him gently, and his length pokes into my abdomen. I want to reach for him, to run my fingers through his hair, but I'm petrified that if I make any sudden movements, I'll scare him off.

His hand runs up my chest painstakingly slowly. His tongue pushes into my mouth, and he opens wider to allow me in. I could cry. His taste is so sweet, like I always knew it would be. He breathes into me, filling my lungs with the oxygen I've been starved of for the last fifteen years.

I move my hand slowly up his side, reaching for the back of his neck. A poor move because the moment my fingers touch his skin, he snaps out of it, flinching and shoving me away with such force that I bounce off the wall behind me.

"Wait!" I call, picking myself off the floor, but it's too late. He's already gone, the office door slamming behind him.

16

Emily

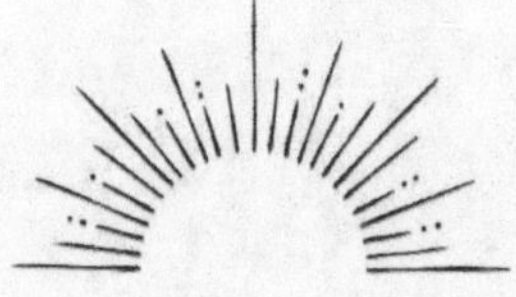

I'm not the gardener. The parish has a man who comes twice a week to tend the fields. The only purpose of my presence in the rows of greens should be to collect herbs and produce for meals. Yet, I continue to find myself amongst the stalks and sprouts, toiling away as if my labor will untangle the threads of worry in my head. And hey, so far, it's working fucking fantastic.

This morning, after I read the slip of paper that flew from under my door. I needed a drink. Alas, there's no liquor cabinet hidden away in the kitchen of a catholic parish, so the garden was my next best option.

I examine my wristwatch to find I've been toiling for two hours already. There goes a big chunk of my time to prepare dinner. Whatever. If Father Robert wants me to make meals for them and then leave while they eat so they aren't in my presence, then he can eat a fucking sandwich every day for all I care. Okay, maybe I do care. I love my job, but it's becoming less and less desirable every time those confusing priest vegetables change their mind about our relationship, and I'm just supposed to be okay with whatever.

I imagine squashing their stupid tomato and cucumbery heads just to show them how much control I actually have in all of this. Okay, that would be murder. I don't want to murder them, but I am raging. I shouldn't be mad at Laurent. It's not his fault that his priestly sidekick has control issues and struggles with admitting his true feelings. Father Robert and Father Laurent signed the note about how our weird vegetable relationship can't continue. Still, the handwriting was the same, and I could tell from the boxy, neat letters that Robert was the sole curator of the declaration.

I sigh, swinging my basket over my shoulder as a bead of sweat runs down my temple. I don't want to head inside yet, but I also can't sit in the sun any longer, at risk of becoming a sweat puddle. The dense forest ahead catches my eyes, and I pick up my step, squelching in my red rubber boots, as I head toward my sanctuary. As I get closer, a melodic sound greats my ears. At first, I'm certain it's the singing of birds mixed with a windchime in the distance, but as I get closer, I notice the guitar strings and a sweet, low voice.

I follow the sound, stepping over tree roots and ducking under low-hanging branches. The musician's words get louder. He's just on the other side of a trunk when I hear, "Everybody wants a water buffalo. Yours is mean, but mine is a kind fellow. Oh, where would you find one? I don't know, but everybody wants a water buffalo."

I choke on my laughter, covering my mouth with my hands.

The music stops. "Are you here to murder me?"

"It's Emily, Laurent."

"The question still stands."

I move around the trunk, staring down at him at the tree's base. He looks up at me with humor-glinted eyes. "Why would I murder you?" I sit next to him, crossing my legs in front of me.

"Because you followed me out in the woods where no one can hear me scream."

I smirk, shaking my head. "I wasn't following you. It's just a happy coincidence."

He leans in, whispering. "So you're happy we're alone together in the woods. I was being truthful. No one could hear our screams out here."

"Laurent!" I push him back, even as my cheeks redden and my core clenches.

"I'm sorry. I can't help myself sometimes." He places his guitar on the ground, turning to face me fully.

"What are you doing out here anyways?" I take in his outfit. "And what are you wearing?"

He looks down at his baby-blue sweater with a bright yellow ducky stitched to the front. "This was a present from one of our patrons, thank you very much. Sure, a rubber ducky is an odd choice for a sweater for a grown man, but it's quite soft."

I cross my arms. My cheeks strain from my grin. "And what are you doing? Why are you singing about water buffalos?"

"Sometimes I like to write kids' songs. I figured one day I could have a special during church called 'Silly Songs with Laurent.'" He smiles, and his eyes shine.

"But I don't think there's any children in the congregation. Is there?"

He sighs. "Sadly, no. But maybe with the right music choice..." He tilts his head to the side.

"Ah, I see, great thinking."

He yawns and throws his arms overhead, his sweater revealing a section of hardened abs. To think I've let these men explore my most sensitive spots, and this is the first time I've gotten a glimpse of his exposed skin. Well, at least his human skin. None of this is fair.

"So, if you're not here to murder me. Why are *you* out here?"

I remember my anger and cross my arms over my chest. "I'm pouting. In fact, I'm thinking of ways to make you and Robert's life more difficult."

He places a hand on his chest and scoots closer to me. "Me? What did I do?"

"The note?"

"What note?"

My suspicions were correct. "Ah. So I guess Daddy Robert has decided this is over for all of us, huh?"

He sighs, running a hand across his temple. "Did he break up our vegetable fun with a note and sign my name?"

I rustle around in my pocket, pulling out the note. "Yep!" I hand it to him.

His eyes scan over the paper, and he gives a forced laugh. "That fucker."

"Listen, I understand. This is weird, and you two are priests, but the back-and-forth is getting annoying. It just seems like I don't have a say in any of this. No one asked me if God came to me in a dream and told me why this is all happening."

Laurent peers over the letter at me. "Did he? Come to you in a dream."

"Well, no."

He shakes his head, returning his attention to the letter. "Me either. In fact, he never really speaks to me."

A thought dawns on me. I look at watch. "Hey, it's been like ten minutes of us alone, and you still haven't turned into a cucumber."

Laurent examines himself. "Look at that. I guess it is only when all three of us are together."

"I wonder why, though."

"Don't think about it too much. I don't think any of this is supposed to make sense." He has a point. This magic doesn't seem to be defined by logic.

I subconsciously scoot closer, wanting to feel Laurent's warmth. It was hot in the field, but here in the shade of the forest, a chill runs over my exposed skin. "I don't get you."

"What do you mean?" he asks, returning to reading over the letter as if he'll discover the key to some cryptic message.

"Why does it feel like you don't believe in all of this—abstinence, priesthood, God?"

His eyes meet mine, and he places the letter by his side. He sighs and lies on his back, propping his head in his hands. "How can any of us be sure of anything?"

I lie next to him, turning on my side to study him. "But you've dedicated your whole life to this? Why would you do that if you're unsure?"

He turns, mimicking my posture. His expression grows serious, the light in his eyes fading. "I think you know why."

I do. I'd be blind not to notice it. He's in love with Robert. I can't blame him. It's hard not to be pulled in by his good looks and domineering presence. But while Robert is tragically beautiful, Laurent is on another spectrum. He's like a Greek god, filled with light that shines through his chiseled features. He's so easy to be around—sucking you in as if every word is a secret just for you—like you're the most important person in the universe. How could Robert not be in love with Laurent? Maybe he doesn't see it yet. They're priests, after all—it's much more complicated than just admitting what your heart wants.

And then here I am. A random girl, rubbing their vegetable bodies all over me like a horny teenager. Their love story seems poetic and tragic—like Achilles and Patroclus but adding me to the mix makes it seem like some corny smut novel. Maybe that's what attracted me to them originally—this weird connection between the two. I can't help but want to be around them, alone, but especially when they're together. They irritate and excite me, each in their own way.

Laurent's gaze locks into mine—intense and wanting. Does he wish I was Robert? Maybe I wouldn't care. I don't want to break the thick silence between us. My heart beats faster, and anticipation that something is about to happen crawls over me, but I can't help words from slipping from my lips. "Let's pretend that you're the boss, not Robert. What would you do about all of this?"

His eyes lock in on my lips. "I'd start with kissing you."

I gulp, my saliva sticky down my throat. "What would Robert say about that?" My breath heavies, and my eyelids flutter. He reaches for me, grabbing the back of my neck. "Fuck, Robert." He crashes his lips into mine.

My body lights up like someone dropped fireworks into my bloodstream. His tongue pushes its way between my parted lips, and he pulls me closer until our bodies are pressed together amongst the blanket of fallen leaves around us. I've had this man inside me—well, in his cucumber form, but this simple kiss is so much more intimate than anything I've experienced with him. He's a priest—a human with flesh and blood. He's disobeying God—breaking his vows, all to place his lips on mine. My stomach flutters at the thought.

I push back, my hands on his chest. "You were right."

He searches my expression, alarmed at my suddenness to stop the kiss. "What?"

"Your sweater. It's *really* soft."

His face lights up, and for a moment, I catch that sparkle that resembles when he looks at Robert. Maybe it's my eyes playing tricks on me—a misplaced beam of light shining through the brush overhead. He laughs, shaking his head before pushing my back to the ground and hovering over me as he kisses me.

I wonder how many women he's been with. He knows what he's doing—nipping at my lips and moving his tongue as if I'm the sweetest taste. He unbuttons my blouse, starting from the bottom and working his way up, not even needing to pause to monitor his work. I moan into his mouth once his large hands work up my abdomen—slow and steady.

My hands trail up his back, under his sweater. Underneath him, I feel so small and delicate—an unusual occurrence between us since the other two times, he was so much smaller than me.

He pulls his lips away from mine and leans his lips to my ear. "My sweater doesn't even hold a candle to the softness of your skin."

I smile into his hair.

"God, Emily. I've waited so long to touch you like this. Is this heaven?"

I grab his face, pulling his mouth back to mine. His hands move up my body, hesitating for a moment once he reaches the ridge of my breast. I buck into him, urging him to touch me there. I want him all over me. Everywhere.

His hand grazes over my nipple, and he turns his head away, sucking in a shaky breath. "Emily, you'll have to forgive me. It's been so long."

I love him saying my name—the way it sounds so tortured on his lips.

"It's only been a day." I retort. He locks his gaze on me and gives me a protruded lip. He gives me a sidelong look. "Pounding you as produce doesn't even compare to how I can fuck you. I'm in control of your pleasure this time."

"Oh, so you're in control now. And what am I? A voiceless bystander." I smirk.

He grinds his body against me so I can feel his erection through his slacks. He lowers himself, his head at my breast, his hands still caressing my skin. "I'm here to worship you, Emily. You are a goddess at the altar." His dark and hungry eyes leave mine before trailing a kiss down my abdomen and unbuttoning my jeans. He sits up on his knees and yanks his sweater off. Thank God. I didn't want to fuck a man in a rubber ducky sweater. Besides, I've been dying to see what the hardness I've only ever felt and imagined looked like. He's lean, muscular, and tan. His abs are like an arrow pointing below his slacks.

I want him to take off more, but before I can ask, he yanks my pants off in one swoop. I shriek, alarmed by his strength and the chill nipping my goosebumped legs. He lowers his head between my legs, breathing over my panties. I shudder.

"You're soaking these through, Emily." He pulls my underwear to the side, running his finger gently along my seam. "God, you're so wet. I was worried you only wanted me as a cucumber."

I can't form words. He's so gentle, and every small movement makes me want to melt out of my skin. He lowers his lips, stroking me softly with his tongue. He inhales sharply, pulling away and turning his head. "Fuck, you taste so good. The sweetest fruit." He returns his attention to me, picking up my ass and sliding my soaking panties down my legs.

I'm bare on the forest floor—my shirt completely open and my ass grinding against the ground. He's moving too slowly—it's wonderful but also torturous. I buck my hips, needing more of him. He pushes me down, his thumb pressing into my hips, as he inserts his tongue deeper into me, lapping up and down but avoiding my clit and my entrance. He knows what he's doing—this teasing game, bringing me so close to the edge even before he's started.

"Laurent!" I yell, my voice is airy and strained. "I need more."

"Shhh," he whispers against my cunt. "I'm savoring you. Let me have my fill first."

I grab his wild hair, urging him to move fast, hard, more direct on my pleasure points, but he's stronger than me and continues his lazy strokes, moaning softly. His pants jingle, and he rustles with the fabric. I sit up, raising myself to my elbows to watch as he pushes his pants and underwear down and reaches for his cock. He strokes himself, tugging desperately as if he can't last another minute without the friction. He's large, much like the size of him as a cucumber. Just the sight of his glistening dick brings me closer, and the need to release is urgent.

"Please, Laurent," I beg, throwing my head back as the sight becomes too much.

Finally, he heeds my request, focusing on my clit and flicking it up and down with pressure and consistency. God, does he know what he's doing. What a shame that this man has gone years without bringing a woman pleasure. It only takes a few strokes before I spiral—my nerves exploding throughout my body and the bliss washing over me like a tidal wave. I grab onto his hair as I ride his face. He doesn't stop as I buck against him, ringing out every last ounce of my orgasm.

I fall back to the Earth, catching my breath as I stare up at the white clouds poking through the shade of branches. I'm dizzy with ecstasy, but Laurent kissing up my legs and venturing up my body brings me back to the moment.

He drags his body over mine, and I reach for him, moving my hands over the muscular expanse of his back. He kicks his pants and boxers off gracefully, his dick rubbing up my body, wetting my skin. He kisses my breasts, flicking his tongue over my pebbled nipples, and it's like my orgasm was years ago. My body sings with arousal, and I'm desperate for more. He pulls himself away from me, his eyes clenching as he sucks in a breath as if using every ounce of his reserve not to lose himself before planting his lips back on my skin.

He takes his time, kissing me as if he's savoring me, but I'm not as patient. I attempt to pull him up to me, needing his lips on mine, needing him inside of me. He heeds my silent request, dragging himself the rest of the way up, planting pained kisses in his wake. He kisses my lips hungrily, his breath heaving in his chest. I writhe against him, urging him to drive inside of me—needing all of him.

He lowers his lips to my ear. "I don't know how long I'll last. I'm sorry."

"No, that's so fucking hot." Of course, I'd want him to pound into me for hours, but the thought that this Greek god of a man is so turned on by me that he's about to sputter out of control, flings me close to the edge again. I've never felt so powerful, so wanted.

He reaches down, positioning himself at my entrance before pushing his tip in. "Fuck!" he yells. I'm so wet that I make way for him, but I can't deny the stretching due to his size. I don't think I'd be able to take him so easily if it wasn't for my practice with him in his cucumber form. He slowly pushes himself in, deeper and deeper. I cry out, my nails digging into his skin. He's so muscular that his abs rub against my sensitive clit.

"I'm so close," he says, his voice cracking.

"Fill me, Father."

He said he had the power this time, but it's like my words granted him permission. He makes one last strong thrust, his mouth snapping open as he moans. The sight of him over me, so lost in himself, sends me spiraling after him—the second orgasm even more powerful than the first. He makes tiny thrusts, and I feel his release seeping out of me. I can't help but wonder when the last time he came was. It feels like there's enough semen built up from a long time.

I rub his back as we catch our breaths, his head resting in the crook of my neck, feeling his heartbeat slow against me. He distributes most of his weight on his knees and hands so he doesn't crush me, but he drapes over me as if he never wants to move. I play with the coarse strands of his hair. They feel like he's spent all day at the beach—as if he's covered in the salty air. I could lay like this forever, but I feel his stomach rumble against mine and remember that it's my job to feed him—him and Robert.

I want to enjoy this soft moment with him, listen to the birds chirp overhead, and imagine I could be enough for Laurent, but reality settles over me. I just fucked a priest and not a transformed priest as a vegetable. If there's a hell, I definitely have a special place in it. What does this mean for all of us, and what happens next?

17

Robert

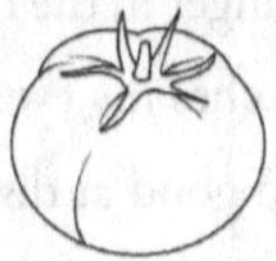

"**F**uck," I mutter as I notice the blood dripping down my fingers. I thought I'd conquered the nasty habit of biting my nails, but here I am with jagged, nubby fingers and a bleeding nail bed. After Laurent kissed me, I ran from him, wrote a note to Emily ending everything, and shoved myself into my work to bury the dirty thoughts. Even though I've been able to keep myself distracted, it seems my subconscious habit is rearing its ugly head.

I rummage through my desk drawers, searching for a bandage. Thankfully, there's one tucked in at the back corner of my bottom drawer. I didn't want to leave my office, where I have barricaded myself for the past two days. Emily or Laurent could be out there, and I'm not strong enough to deal with either.

Gail returns from vacation soon. I need to hide from the two until she's back. Another person will wade through the tension and remind us that someone is watching. At least, that's what I hope. I want to pretend the last few days never happened. Maybe if I'm not around Laurent and Emily, I don't even have to worry about becoming a vegetable again. Somehow, turning into a vegetable is the least terrifying part of this. Facing my problems head-on? Yeah, I'd rather be a nutritious snack.

As I wrap my injured finger in the tan bandage, the clock on the corner of my desk catches my eye. "Damn, it's five o'clock already?" I've always been good at distracting myself from my feelings. Who needs to deal with their inner demons when you can drown yourself in work or God?

I sigh, staring out the cracked window to my left. The sun sits low in the sky, casting an orange blanket on the rolling, green hills. Usually, the sight would cause me to praise the Lord and marvel at his creation, but right now, it pisses me off. Everything has a place, a job, and acts in perfect order. The trees don't worry about whether or not they want to be a tree or if they have feelings for a bush. The grass doesn't get distracted or forget to cover the earth. Why would God make personhood so difficult? Why would he leave so many questions unanswered and only up for interpretation? If he cared so much about good and evil, wouldn't he clarify what is truly evil and what isn't?

I shake my head. I need to get back to work. These are the type of thoughts I'm attempting to avoid, and I can't even look outside of my fucking window without them crawling around the ridges of my brain.

Before I divert my attention back to the scramble of papers before me, something catches my eye in the distance at the edge of the field. Emily jumps at the base of a large oak tree. Her grunts and aggravated yells carry to my office. Even from this distance, the sight of her sends warmness through my body. Her brown hair blowing in the breeze, the way her breasts and ass stick out from the side. Without even trying, her form is erotic and sinful, something I want to conquer, something I want to cherish and worship. Why would God send her here—a beautiful woman who makes me feel things I've never had to worry about?

Emily stops jumping, looking up at the large tree before pressing her body against it and swinging a foot onto a knobby post near the bottom. She moves higher, slowly, and wobbly, proving she has no business climbing a tree.

"Goddammit," I mutter. She will break her neck if she climbs any higher. I sigh, standing and exiting my office.

"What the fuck are you doing?" I yell once I'm still a hundred feet away from her, stomping over a small hill. I didn't want to sneak up and send her tumbling out of the tree, so I made my presence known farther away.

She whips her attention to me, almost losing her grip on a branch but quickly regaining control. She shakes her head. "No. No, you don't get to yell things like that at me."

I'm closer now, but I still raise my voice. "Are you trying to injure yourself so you get workman's comp? Gail should have gone over that with you. We don't offer it."

She gives an aggravated grunt. She's angry, a side of her I've never witnessed before. "You're a priest, remember? You're supposed to be nice to me—Godly and shit. You can't swear and yell and insult my intelligence," she yells, her face red as she looks down at me. She's not high up in the tree. I could easily pull her down, but it sure as hell took her a long time to get this far.

I ignore her comment. She's obviously frustrated and taking it out on me, even if what she said is true and makes me feel guilty. I place my hands on my hips, shaking my head as I gaze up at her. I sigh and soften my tone, "Emily, what are you doing? You're going to hurt yourself."

She points over her head to one of the high branches. "My hat! It flew off my head and got caught in the branches," she yells down at me.

"Okay, well, let me get it. You obviously don't know what you're doing." I extend my hand for her to grab hold.

"No. Fuck off."

I sigh, and my cock twitches in my slacks at her brattiness, which aggravates and excites me further. "I'm just trying to help."

She glares at me. "You know, you suck at offering help. You make it feel like an insult."

I spit a short laugh, her candor making me forget myself for a moment. "I apologize. You're scaring me, and I get rash when I'm worried."

She scoffs but studies me, her chest heaving from the short climb. "Fine. I'd rather you break your neck than me."

I chuckle as she steps backward, and I position my body under hers. "Okay, now step back on that branch," I direct with my words, hoping to get her down safely without touching her. My cock and mind won't be able to take it.

My presence must instill confidence in her because she steps back without caution, missing the branch entirely. She screeches as she falls from the tree and into my arms. The air escapes from my lungs, and I fall backward, not anticipating the force.

"Oh, my god. Are you okay?" She rolls off me, lying at my side as she props herself up and examines me.

I wince, my eyes clenched shut. "I'm fine," I wheeze, oxygen not fully returned to my lungs.

Her hands run up my abdomen and arms until she cups my cheeks. "I'm sorry. Does it hurt anywhere?" Suddenly, no pain exists in my body. My skin sizzles under her touch, and I keep my eyes closed, wanting to live under her fingertips forever.

"Robert, are you okay?" she asks again when my silence lasts too long.

"I'm fine." I open my eyes, catching her chocolate ones just above me. Now it's her who's silent. Her lips part, and her breath hitches. It would be so easy to fulfill my desires, even with my bruised ribs. I could wrap my hand around her neck and pull her into my lips. I could explore her mouth with my tongue, let my hands wander under her light shirt, and roll around until our clothes fall off and we've given ourselves completely to each other. She would welcome it. Every inch of her skin begs me to touch her and lick her and fuck her.

Her eyes flutter closed, and she inches closer subtly. She's about to kiss me. She wants this so bad that she doesn't care about my note or that I'm a priest. God, do I want her to do it, but my guilt runs deeper, deeper than my lust.

"Do you really need that hat?" I break the spell. She jerks away from my lips, sitting upright.

"What?"

I point to the woven fabric still dancing in the branches. "Can you live without it?"

She sighs, staring at it. "I guess so. I'm used to living without things I want." I don't know if she means to make me feel sorry for her, but it works. My heart breaks. I ignore my aches and pains, jumping to my feet and charging the oak.

"Robert, no. Really. It's fine. I have other hats."

I ignore her, grabbing the nearest branch and pulling myself up, swinging my legs as I rise higher.

"Holy shit. You're like a spider monkey."

I laugh at her words but continue my climb, sweat tickling my temple as I grab the hat and scale back down the way I came. I jump to the grass and wince in pain at the impact. Normally, jumping down wouldn't hurt, but I did just have an adult woman fall on top of me.

"Why are you so good at climbing trees?" Emily asks, stepping in front of me and placing her hands on the hat in mine.

I shake my head. "How about a thank you, Father Robert?"

She rolls her eyes, our hands still connected by the straw hat. "Thank you, Father," she says Father slowly, her top teeth grazing against her plump bottom lip. She smirks.

I sigh. "Fuck off." I turn away, rubbing my hand down my face.

"What? I said thank you."

"I know what you said. You can't say Father like it turns you on."

She holds her hands up as if dropping any blame. "I think you're projecting."

I can't help but laugh. She smiles at me, her eyes sparkling. I can read the words, "I finally got you," off her smug expression. I want to kiss it off her face. *Fuck. No.* I can't think like that. I compose myself and turn back to the parish, ready to return to my office and pray to God for forgiveness until my knees bleed.

Emily rushes to catch up with me. "So, tell me. Why are you so good at climbing trees?"

I keep my gaze straight ahead as we walk side by side. "Because I climb trees often."

"You do?"

"Yes, I have other hobbies besides being a priest."

"Like what?"

"I don't know." I think for a second. "I like to make things."

"Things?" Her hands clasp behind her back and she leans forward to get a better look at my face.

"Like woodworking. I built the kitchen table."

"Wow, that's impressive!"

I blush. "But I don't have a lot of time to do it."

"I see."

A silence washes over us. I should be glad for it. Talking with Emily is a bad idea, but I realize I barely know anything about her. I've rolled over her naked flesh and watched her melt into ecstasy, but I don't even know what she does for fun. "What about you?"

"What about me?"

"What are your hobbies?"

She is silent, and I watch her stare at the cloud in thought. Her loose braid bounces against her back, and baby hair wisps over the freckles speckling her temple. "I guess I don't really have hobbies."

"That can't be true."

"No, really. I was in a long relationship where I lost myself. He was abusive. Not physically, but verbally and financially. He cut me off from my friends and family, and I wasn't allowed to work or drive. My only hobbies then were frequenting dive bars with him and making sure our mobile home was perfectly clean and there was a hot meal on the table before he got home from work. I guess I kind of lost myself all those years."

I stop, grabbing her arm. "Oh, Emily. I'm sorry. I didn't mean to..."

She waves me off. "No, it's fine. It doesn't make me sad to talk about it. I'm much happier here. I guess I'm learning to garden, which I like. I've always loved to cook, but I love it more now that I don't have to cook for an asshole." She laughs, but I tense, my mind replaying my behavior toward her over the last week. Did Emily just escape one asshole to work for another? Maybe I'm even worse because I'm pretending to be good—Godly even.

"Emily, I'm so sorry."

"No, really, it's fine. I don't have to worry about him anymore. I even heard he got arrested for a DUI last week, so he'll be sitting in jail for a while." She laughs. "He's an idiot."

"No, I'm not talking about your ex. I mean with Laurent and me. We never should have taken advantage of you the way we did."

She scrunches her brow. "You didn't take advantage of me. I wanted it. You were sentient objects, and I was the one making all the moves. Just because I left an abusive relationship doesn't mean I can't make my own choices."

"No, but we're authoritative figures, ordained by God. We should be helping you. Not using you for our own gain."

She clenches her fist. "Robert, you were a tomato I rubbed myself off with. Be so for real right now." She turns away from me, her arms over her chest.

I rest my hand on her shoulder. "I promise nothing between us three will ever happen again. Not even as vegetables."

She whips back to me, her face red and scowling. "You don't get to decide everything. What if something already happened again, and you couldn't stop it?"

My heart drops. "What do you mean?"

"You don't control Laurent and me. We can make our own choices."

I grab her wrist, anger clouding my vision. "Did something happen between you two?"

She shakes her hand, trying to slip free of my grasp, but I don't let up. Seconds ago, I apologized to her, but that regretful man is gone. Now, I want answers.

"Maybe." She stares me down.

I breathe out through my nose. "Emily, I need an answer."

"Why? Would you get angry at me for messing around with the love of your life?"

I drop her hand. "What are you talking about?"

"I know you love him, just as much, if not more than he loves you. You can hide it all you want, but if you hold it inside much longer, you will do something you regret."

"You don't know what you're talking about."

I turn away from her, stomping to the kitchen door. She catches up to me and grabs my wrist. I whirl around, facing her, our chests against each other. "So what is it? Is it him or me you are jealous of?"

I glare down at her, my breath heaving in my chest. I want to run and hide and pray, but with her this close, I can't control my thoughts. Her question is one I can't answer. Do I feel jealousy? Yes, it's there, but I don't know who it's directed toward. If anything, I just feel left out. Maybe I should make this right, even the playing field. I lower my head quickly before I can talk myself out of it and capture Emily's lips with mine.

She gasps into me as I grab the back of her neck, pulling her into me. My tongue explores her mouth, and I moan at the taste of her. I wonder how long it had been since Laurent's mouth was on her. I bite her lip, and she screams, pushing me back.

Her lip is already red with a small bubble of blood. She pats it with her hand, looking at me in confusion.

"No more," I say, no humor in my voice, before turning and charging inside, pushing my erection out of my way.

18

Emily

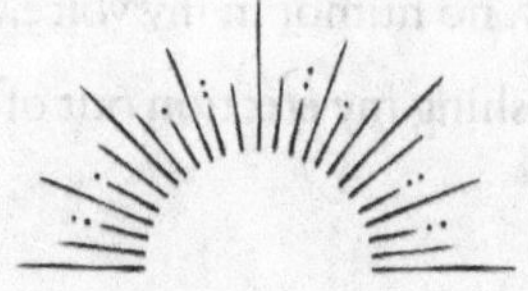

My haven has become an impenetrable labyrinth. I can't face Laurent, and I definitely can't face Robert after that confusing kiss. I'm not sure what I want because it doesn't seem to matter. Even if I decided, I couldn't have it.

Maybe Laurent and I could run away together. Live in a quaint house in the countryside with just each other's company. I could be happy with him. It's not that I need a man, but Laurent makes life sweeter—more fun and joyful. I smile to myself in the darkness of my room, imagining waking to Laurent's sleepy smile, making pancakes together, and wiping batter across each other's face. I try to elongate the scene, but it's blurry. It would be happy, but it wouldn't work. There would always be something missing between us.

Robert's dark eyes come to mind, watching Laurent and me sternly. I shiver, my quilt comforter not enough to warm me. It's obvious. I want them both—different and desperately. And not just as stupid fucking vegetables. Thinking about everything that's happened between the three of us over the past few days makes the whole vegetable situation seem ridiculous. Who cares that Robert doesn't want me to use them to pleasure myself when they're a cucumber and tomato? It wouldn't be enough for me now.

That's not true, though. If Robert gave me even an inch, I would take it. Now I know how Laurent must have felt over all these years—living off Robert's scraps.

This isn't my fault. I didn't ask for them to turn into produce and radiate a magnetic sexual energy. I didn't beg Laurent to fuck me on the forest floor or for Robert to kiss me and then bite me. Of course, I wanted all those things while they were happening, but everyone involved was an equal participant. Laurent and Robert are big priests. They make their own decisions. But I can't help feeling guilty. They had a life together before I arrived. Sure, it was filled with masked secrets and living off stolen touches, but it was something. I come in and mess everything up, forcing them to face their feelings. Knowing Robert, though, he'll keep hiding as long as he can. I just don't think it will be enough for Laurent anymore.

I grunt, sitting up and throwing my legs over the side of my bed. For a quiet country parish, I sure have a hard time falling asleep. I pick up the clock on my bedside table. It's two in the morning. I'll take a walk around the property to tire myself out. No one should be awake now, so I don't need to worry about walking in on either of the priests. I've done a good job avoiding them all day and want to keep it up.

I pull a sweater over my oversized t-shirt and sleep shorts, step into my boots, and exit my room. I pause, listening to hear if anyone's up. It's silent, and I descend from the living quarters into the night.

Cicadas and frogs sing around me. An owl hoots in the distance. Finally, some noise distracts my thoughts. My thin sweater isn't warm enough, though. I don't want to head back to my room or the kitchen to happen upon one of the men. The chapel in the distance catches my eye. Maybe it will be open, and I can hide out. Maybe I can even get some answers from God.

I shove one of the large, ornate double doors when I reach the entrance. I strain under its weight, but it creeps open. I continue pushing until a me-sized crack forms, and I slip through. The warmth hits me as I enter, and I turn to shut the door behind me, not wanting the chill to seep in. It's quiet—deathly quiet, and I sigh, annoyed that I must be alone with my thoughts again. I guess it's time to talk to ol' daddy God. I eye the pews, and my dream from many nights before comes to mind—Father Robert standing before me, about to whip his dick from his pants, Father Laurent at my side, rubbing his cucumber cock against my skin. I take a shaky breath. Yeah, I'm gonna skip the pews.

A brown closet to my right catches my eye. It's a confessional booth. I've seen them on TV, but never in real life. The thought of confessing my sins out loud to a stranger who can't see my face has always seemed cathartic, but I know both of the priests that could be on the other side—a little too well. Now that it's empty, though, I could pretend there's someone on the other end who won't judge me. This seems like the perfect place to absolve my sins.

I step into the wooden cubby and sit on the firm bench. I thought it would be smaller, but I'm surprised I have ample legroom. These things are designed for people much larger than five feet three inches, after all.

I close my eyes, breathing deeply, gathering my words. "Forgive me, Father, for I have sinned." Shit, that sounded legit. I can't believe I remembered that line from TV. Maybe I should come back when one of the priests is here so I can show off my Catholic skills. The thought of Laurent or Robert sitting on the other side of this box sends a heatwave to my core. My mind plays images of their low voices directing me how to atone for my sins—to get on my knees for them. *Fuck.* Daddy God would not like where my mind is right now.

I clear my throat. "Anyways. I think I've sinned a lot recently. I'm not sure. I haven't read the Bible before. Maybe that's a sin. So mark that down. Yeah, sorry about that. I'll get right on it." I pause for a second. "Actually, no, I won't. That book is way too long and boring. I guess I'm sorry for lying about going to read the Bible. Anyways, ugh. Let's get back on track."

This may be harder than I thought. I drop my head, staring up at the dark ceiling. "It's just these two priests. They're messing with my head. I want them so bad. Like biblically. It started as just a harmless crush. Then you went ahead and turned them into vegetables, and everything got a lot more complicated. Unless you didn't turn them into vegetables, and that's someone else's doing. But if that's the case, I'm not really talking to you right now. I'm probably talking to no one." I sigh. Why did I think this would be a good idea? I'm just praying myself into a hole. Wait, am I even praying or talking to an imaginary priest in a confessional booth? I'm more confused than when I entered this stupid box.

I'm about to abandon this confessional mission and sit alone with my thoughts. "I just need someone to tell me what to do."

"On your knees."

My heart stops. I can't pretend it's God on the other side of the divider. I can't even pretend it's the devil because I know that voice—the dark, husky tone directly from my dreams. I don't move, waiting to see if my mind's playing tricks on me—imagining what I desperately wish to be true.

"Wha…"

"On your knees." He's impatient, his voice gravely and low, just above a whisper, but with enough power behind it to get me to do a backflip.

I drop to the wooden floor beneath me, my heart starting up again and beating thunderously. The door opens on the other side, and footsteps sound until they stop at the door on my side. I clutch my eyes close as my door swings open.

It's dark, so it takes my eyes a second to adjust. He stands before me wearing a black shirt and slacks, his white collar contracting the darkness around him. He stares down at me, his curly locks dangling above his full eyebrows. From the way he's gripping the doorway, his forearms popping with veins, and the scowl on his face, I know I'm in trouble.

"I didn't know anyone was here." My voice cracks.

"Don't speak." He doesn't turn away from me. "You said you wanted someone to tell you what to do, so here I am."

Is this the part where he tells me I'm fired and to get the hell out of here?

"Here's what's going to happen." His hand moves to his belt buckle. "You're going to stay right there, and I'm going to fill you, just as you've been begging me to do with your eyes all these days."

Okay, I'm dreaming. I have to be dreaming.

He pulls his belt off and tugs at his zipper.

"No more talking. Your mouth has brought me to the edge of my control, and these are the consequences."

God, this feels so real. I nod, inching closer to him on my knees. "Yes, Father."

He hisses, turning his head away from me, his hand on his cock still covered by his boxers. The low lights from candles barely illuminate his form before me. He turns his head back toward me, keeping his eyes clenched. "I can't tell if you're sent from God or the devil."

I rise, grabbing his hand that is clutching his cock. "What turns you on more?" He moves his hand away, and I dive under his gray boxers, his skin searing my hand. He hisses again and throws his head back. He wanted to play this differently—be the authoritative figure that told me what to do, and he did so well, my panties soaked completely through, but he's over-estimated himself. He wants this as much, if not more, than me. This is forbidden for him, for me; it's just getting what I've been craving and waiting for him to offer me. I'm about to make him come his brains out.

I pull his boxers down, springing his dick free. It's deliciously hard and long and could rearrange my organs if he fucked me to his hilt. My mouth waters, and I lick my lips. I reach for him, but before I meet his skin, he grabs my wrists. "You've tortured me enough. You'll take me until you're praying to God and asking for forgiveness. This is the atonement for your sins." He grabs the back of my head and fucks my open mouth, hitting the back of my throat. I gag, rearing back, but he doesn't let up, holding me tighter and continuing to drive himself between my lips.

How does he know I like this? He's practically forcing himself on me, but I fucking love it. Isn't he supposed to be good? How does he know I want him to take me so goddamn bad? Oh, right, my hands are currently inside my sleep shorts and strumming my slick clit as if it's a guitar. That's probably a bit telling.

"Fuck!" He slows, holding himself back. I swirl my tongue around his dick, wanting him to keep going, to come inside my mouth.

"Jesus Christ, you like this, don't you? You like being on your knees—worshipping me with my dick in your mouth."

I moan and nod, my eyes watering and my fingers moving frantically. I'm so close to coming. He grabs the back of my neck, hunching over as he spears my mouth. "You're taking me so good, Emily." He seethes through clenched teeth. "Show me how good you are. Swallow me."

I slow my pace on my clit, my fingers just brushing my bundle of nerves. I want to come with him. He's so close. I feel it in his forced and frantic thrusts into me. He probably hasn't come in a long time, as a human at least. He's too devoted to God to falter. Except right now—with me. I'm making him sin, come undone, and abandon his vows. Something Laurent hasn't been able to do. Maybe Robert and Laurent love each other. Maybe I'll never be able to compare to their connection, but here I am with Robert's dick down my throat, bringing him to the edge. He couldn't resist me. His life devotion crumbling to pieces.

I should feel guilt for leading him astray. Maybe I was sent by the devil because all I feel is pure, unadulterated power zipping through my body.

"Oh, God!" Robert cries, releasing into me, his hips jerking as he sputters out of control. The taste of him is so sweet. There's so much, hot and sticky, pouring down my throat.

I've made both of these men come inside of me. They're unable to resist the connection between us. I fucking love the thought, and I moan as my orgasm climbs up my spine. I'm knocked to another dimension. My skin tingles, and my body contracts. I moan around Robert's cock, swallowing every ounce of him.

He holds himself up, his arms extending and leaning against the wall behind me. He catches his breath, and his eyes close. I stare up at him. He's so beautiful when he's sated. God, he's a piece of art. I wish I could see both Laurent and him like this at the same time. The thought doesn't seem too impossible to me now.

Robert's eyes widened, and he stares down at me. Horror morphs on his face as he catches my sly smile. He pushes himself away from the wall. Fumbling with his pants. "Never again." He says before pushing himself away and stomping toward the church door.

I'm left alone, the taste of his semen in my mouth, my body still relaxed from my release. God, do I feel good, but at the same time, I'm more confused than ever. What have I done? What does this make me?

19

Emily

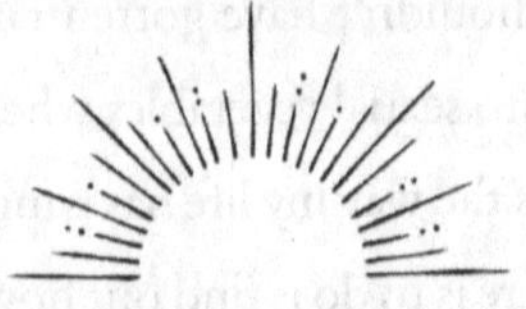

I don't give a fuck what Robert's note said days ago. After what happened last night, I'm not hiding and pushing food under their door. "Dinners ready!" I call before sitting at the head of the table, a steamy bowl of vegetable and roast beef stew in front of me. They can't hide in their rooms forever. We've spent the day avoiding each other, and it ends now. The stew makes my mouth water, and I imagine the fumes seeping under their doors. Hopefully, it's enough to entice them out.

It's not like I want to sit across from the two men I fucked in the last two days, or should I say, the two priests. Last night, when Robert came between my lips, finally giving in to his urges, I felt like a goddess—victorious. When I woke up this morning, my feelings changed. I care about these two men—in a weird, complicated way. Both of them ignite something inside of me I thought I lost forever. My time dating Darrell feels like a lifetime ago, but I'm not the same woman I was under his grasp. The laughter Laurent elicits from me, the fire Robert pulls from my lips—each of them brings out a part of myself I didn't know I still had.

I shouldn't need a man to find myself. I should have more time before jumping into a new relationship–or two at the same time. I definitely shouldn't have gotten tangled up with two priests who turn into sexual vegetables whenever they're in my presence, but this is the way my life has panned out. There's no going back—all there is to do is find out how we go ahead, even if that means we go our separate ways. I lived too many years walking on eggshells. I'm not living that way again.

Laurent's door cracks open. He smiles as he walks to the chair next to me. He sits down, cradles his chin in his hand, and gazes at me. "Smells delicious. Do you think Daddy will join us?"

I chuckle, shaking my head. I should have known this would be easy with Laurent. Everything is easy with him. It's the other one I need to worry about and their confusing relationship.

"If he doesn't leave his room in two minutes, I'm going in there. We need to talk," I say.

Laurent nods before taking a slurp of his soup. "Does he know we fucked?" I choke on my saliva. Of course, this conversation must dive into the fact that I had my own, separate sexual encounter with each of them without being in their vegetable forms. Robert knows—more or less, but I'm not sure how Laurent will take the news. Will he be jealous? Will his cock stiffen, thinking of me tangled up with Robert? I'm both excited and terrified to find out.

I open my lips to answer Laurent's question, but before the words leave my mouth, Robert's door opens, and he walks toward us. His eyes are downcast, and his hair is unruly—not the usual tidiness he displays. He's wearing casual clothes, a grey T-shirt and sleep pants. I shiver. He's not the powerful man who thrust into me last night. He's vulnerable, but the sight doesn't make me want him any less.

He sits, picking up his spoon and dipping it into the stew. Laurent smiles at him. "Wow, I can't believe you're sitting before us."

"I have to eat, don't I?" he replies, not meeting Laurent's gaze.

Laurent sighs and leans back in his chair. "I was just asking Emily if you knew we fucked."

My cheeks heat, and I glare at Laurent. It's true, of course, but right now, I feel like a pawn in their game, like Laurent's just using me to make Robert jealous.

Robert points his spoon at me, still not taking his eyes off the stew. "Did she tell you we fucked?"

"What?" Laurent sits upright, glaring at me with disbelief. "You two fucked?"

"Not technically," I rebuttal. Laurent's expression is wounded. I wonder if he's hurt about me fucking Robert or Robert fucking me. In the moment, I didn't contemplate the other's feelings. We had all three fooled around with them as vegetables. Being with them individually as priests didn't feel too far off.

But now I'm realizing maybe I crossed a line. In fact, I know I crossed a line. I'm just unsure who's.

Laurent turns to Robert. "And you were a man when this happened, not a vegetable?"

"Full man. Priest attire and everything," Robert replies.

Oh yeah, I forgot that Robert nor Laurent turned into their produce self when I moaned around their dicks. The rules of this curse are getting more confusing as time goes on. Maybe what we thought initially was true—they only turn into vegetables when all three of us are together. I wonder how much time we have left to talk before it happens again. It's crazy that the whole vegetable shifting seems like the least of our problems with everything happening. What a fucking mess.

"Same with me," Laurent replies, tapping his fingers on the table and staring Robert down. "Okay, fine. This works. We'll continue as vegetables, and then we can each have a relationship with Emily as humans."

"Wait," I say at the same time that Robert says, "No." Our eyes finally meet. I said wait because I didn't appreciate Laurent making decisions for me without my input. Is that what I want to happen? Kind of, but also, it doesn't feel like enough. Most importantly, I want to have a say in all of this. I want to call at least some of the shots. But now that Robert said no, I'm curious. "No, what?" I ask.

"No. No more of any of us." His brows furrow, and there goes the vulnerable man sitting before me moments ago.

My blood boils. "So now you're telling Laurent and me what to do?"

He grips the table, the veins bulging in his arm. "Yes. Laurent is a priest. He's devoted his life to God. This relationship is inappropriate."

I shoot to my feet. "And what's our relationship then? Was it appropriate last night when your come was sliding down my throat?"

Laurent gives a shrieked laughter; his hand covers his mouth, and his eyes shine.

Robert sighs, running his large hands through his tangles. "That was a misstep, something that will never happen again."

"You sure seem to make a lot of missteps," Laurent replies, twinged with something like annoyance. Robert glares at him.

I can't deny it hurts. No one wants to feel like someone thinks of them as a mistake. I lose my anger and confidence, falling back to my chair. Laurent must notice the change in my demeanor because his voice shifts. "I don't have to be a priest, you know. I can leave the church. I can be with Emily without you." The war on my emotions revs back to life. Does he mean he wants to leave the church to be with me? Or is he using it as a threat?

He stands, walking behind my chair and touching my shoulder. It's like a balm over a burn—his touch soothing me momentarily.

Robert studies us, his eyes darting between ours. "Fine. Leave then." He tries to look uncaring, but he fails miserably. The corner of his lip shakes, and he clenches his fists.

I wonder if Laurent notices it. He travels down my arms and leans over to kiss my neck. His lips linger, kissing lower, and my breath hitches. I can't see his face, but I feel the sexual charge between us. He's wanting something more from me right now. His fingers play at the hem of my shirt, and my stupid fucking breath hitches.

Laurent takes his lips away from my skin. "Tell me you'd be okay with this. Sitting back, watching as I make her mine."

He's silent for a moment but then answers, "I'd be fine." His voice low and gruff and coated with his lie.

Laurent's hand dives underneath the waistband of my skirt. He moves past my underwear and into the already searing heat of my cunt. I cry out, grabbing his other arm and clenching my eyes shut.

"So you won't mind if I take her right here? If I fuck her right here on this table in front of you?"

I open my eyes to watch Robert. I called this dinner to settle reason, to figure out where we all stand. Now, here we all are—exactly where we always end up together, tangling in a web of seduction. Now, I could give a fuck about answers—all except one. I want to know what Robert will do. Will he join us? Will he watch? Will he stomp off to his room in anger? I just pray to any god listening right now that no one turns into a vegetable. I need these men and nothing else.

"Be my guest." The words barely leave his lips, soaking at the edge of his lips. He's still, frozen in place, as his eyes catch mine. It's a warning, a threat, a blessing all in one.

Laurent kisses my neck, his teeth poking through in a smile as he trails. "Want to show him how good you are?" he whispers.

I nod because, of course, I fucking do. No matter how hard I try to be tough and resist these men, to put my foot down and show them who's boss, I never win. My nerves feather. Every touch from Laurent brings me so close to something holy.

He pulls my chair back so Robert can see me better. He yanks my skirt up and my underwear down, revealing me to Robert. My eyelids are heavy, wanting to tune out everything else in the world and focus on the sweet bliss from Laurent's fingertips as he languidly strokes me from my clit to my core, but I can't stop staring at Robert. One hand clenches at his side while the other covers his crotch. He clenches his jaw, his eyes dark, an unruly curl drooping in front of his dilated pupil. I clench my lips, forcing myself not to cry out, to beg him to touch himself as he watches me.

Laurent moves behind my chair, not removing his hand from wringing me of my pleasure. He pulls down the collar of my shirt, exposing my breasts.

"Fuck," Robert whispers, turning his gaze away from me. Power ripples around me, and I cry out as my body blooms like a flower in the morning rays.

"Isn't she so perfect like this? Heaven personified," Laurent says, his voice low as he strums my hardened nipple and my clit.

His words, his movements, Robert's dark and tortured eyes on me as he fumbles with his erection in his pants; it all swirls around me in an aurora borealis of elation. I'm so close to coming.

"Want to guess how many times I can make her come? How many times did you make her come, Robert? I bet I can beat you."

And with that, my body tenses, lava runs up my spine, and I cry out in a muffled whimper. I'm so lost in my bliss that I barely notice the rustling of Robert's pants.

Laurent peppers kisses down my neck as I try to catch my breath. "Do it again." Robert's gruff voice charges something powerful inside of me. My pussy clenches, and my skin prickles with goosebumps. I'm like a live wire, energy running through me again as I watch Robert sitting in his chair facing us. His legs are spread wide, and he grasps his large cock in one hand, taking long, heavy strokes—the veins on his hands engorged as if he's about to choke himself. His eyes are heavy, and his lips are parted. He's no longer anxious or fighting the demon inside of him. He's given himself over to us—ready to wank himself at the sight of this act.

I wait for Laurent's witty remark, but his breath strains, and he seems as lost for words as I am but not in action. He moves quickly, wrapping his arm around my middle and lifting me off the chair. He's standing behind me and whispers in my ear, "Let's put a good show on for him. I want him to know how well you fit around our cocks. It's like you were made for two. How does that sound?"

I nod. "Fuck me, Father."

In one swoop, he pulls my loose white blouse overhead. My breasts burst free, the cool air tickling my flesh. He pushes my front down, bending me over the wooden table. I splay my hands before me, lifting my head to meet Robert's eyes as Laurent hikes up my skirt to my middle. He presses into me, rubbing his hardened length against me, his pants still separating us. Laurent bends over, so tall he has to arch his neck to reach my ear. "I can feel you through my pants. So wet for me–for us."

I bite my lips, my eyes on Robert as his gaze flicks from my eyes to my breasts, pressed against the table and spilling around me. He strokes himself gently, rubbing his palm over his tip before moving up and down. He's so aroused he only needs his own lubrication.

Laurent sticks his finger inside of me. I moan as he inserts two more. "She's taken us both so good. If only you'd let yourself fuck her like this." It happens quickly. He pulls out his fingers, positions his tip at my entrance, and slams into me, his hips slapping against my bare ass.

"Oh, God!" I cry. He's balls deep and even though I've taken him before, I'm not prepared for the size of him. It's deliciously painful, stretching me, and my vision is blurry.

He leans over me again. "I'm your God now," he whispers. "No, that's not true. This pussy is my God." He thrusts into me as he spills words into my ear. "This is what I've been looking for all this time. Your cunt is holier than any religion—more sacred than any altar. I'll worship you until there's nothing left of me, and even after that." His words are beautiful, sinful, and righteous all at the same time. I'm unsure if he's just spewing nonsense—lost in his own lust, or if he means it. I don't mind either way.

He fucks me hard and fast, hitting the back of my walls—the spot that spirals a vortex of pleasure from the base of my spine. I don't take my eyes off Robert's even for a second. His head is thrown back, but his eyes stay open—half-lidded as if it takes every ounce of his energy not to get lost in the sight before him. Laurent isn't the only one speaking these words into my ear or fucking into my cunt. Robert is here with him. This is what I was looking for. No, it's not enough, not even close. I still have so much room for both of them. I want them both inside of me—both on my body, but this will have to do for now. It's so much better than anything I've ever experienced.

I'm so close to coming, watching as Robert meets his edge. He grunts, and his strokes increase in speed, matching Laurent's thrusts from behind. I'm right at the edge, hoping Laurent and Robert topple down with me when someone screams. Not one of us.

Gail stands in the doorway behind me. Her hand covers her mouth, and horror masks her face.

Nobody turned into a vegetable, but this is much, much worse.

20

Laurent

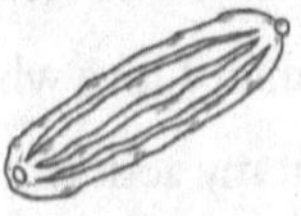

I've imagined what it would be like when everything caught fire. If all the hidden feelings and suppressed urges boiled over and avalanched into our lives here at the parish. I played scenarios where Robert would stop his sermon, turn to me, grab my face, and suck the life out of me before taking my hand and prancing down the aisle. I've imagined a late-night conversation where we confess our feelings and run off into the sunset. My mind constantly wanders with how we could leave this place and be together, but I never thought it would end quite like this.

"I'll be praying for you, men," Archibald says. His eyes pin us in place at the desk. It sounds nice, but in reality, it's a big *fuck you*. He said men, not brothers, not Fathers, just men—which is all we are now, no longer priests. We're probably ex-communicated. We'll have to wait for our trial before the board in a month.

He shakes his head, his eyes judging us more than any words could before shutting the door behind him and leaving us alone. As much as I hated being reprimanded, belittled, threatened with hell, and stripped of the title I'd known and worked for the last fifteen years, I'd rather him not leave. I would rather not be alone with Robert, the man I love who just had his life ripped in two, mostly because of my actions.

He's counting on me now. Whether he admits it or not, the silence is too thick, and we can't turn to face each other. This is my cue—the part where I say something ridiculous and mildly, or completely, inappropriate. I wrack my brain looking for a witty one-liner, one that smooths over all the sharp edges of the last twenty-four hours, but nothing comes to mind. There's too much to say to each other.

When Gail walked in on me fucking Emily from behind while Robert sat in front of us, stroking his cock, she nearly had a heart attack. I can't blame her. Every time I catch a glimpse of Emily's tits or Robert's dick, I nearly pass out too. She wasn't even expecting it.

Gail left the kitchen as quickly as she came, and after we fumbled to dress ourselves, Robert ran after her. I followed just a little behind, staying far enough away to hear but not to be seen. Gail didn't want to discuss it and told Robert she should resign. Robert wouldn't have it. He told her that this wasn't her fault; it was his. Really, it was more mine, but I wasn't about to jump in and offer my guilt. He would call the archbishop that night, tell him what happened, and resign from his position.

When Robert finished speaking with Gail, I approached him, wanting to discuss everything that had happened and what to do now. He wouldn't even look at me. I searched his face for anger or sadness, but I found nothing. He walked past me, past Emily waiting in the kitchen, and returned to his room, locking the door behind him.

I comforted Emily and told her what Robert had said to Gail and that we'd figure this out in the morning. She was rattled–embarrassed, and her face guilt-ridden. I kissed her on the cheek goodnight and returned to my room, hoping someone would visit me in the middle of the night.

This morning, I woke to a note under my door. A neat and tight script informed me we'd meet with Archibald first thing and meet in the chapel office. Robert didn't say a word to me, and now, as I stand at the edge of the desk searching for something to say, he remains silent. The last time we were in this office alone, we shared our first and last kiss. This place is holy, even if Robert's uncertainty tries to taint it.

Maybe I do believe in God because, finally, he clears his throat and speaks. "I'm going to become a monk. I found a monastery on a remote island off the coast. I leave tomorrow."

Just kidding. God is a cruel bastard.

"What happens if you turn into a tomato in front of the monks?" It's odd. Our vegetable curse hasn't come to mind until now. Even last night, I barely questioned why we stayed human while in the act. Every time before, it seemed to be the key to our transformation. Maybe this time was different. Maybe our curse was broken. I doubt it. Nothing felt new or changed. It felt like the same place we've been for the last fifteen years, except much worse.

"Then maybe, God willing, the monks will eat me, and my misery will be over."

"Oh, for fuck's sake, Robert, quit with the dramatics. You don't need to become a monk."

He turns to me, his eyes catching mine, and it's like a snow truck dumps a pile of slush on my soul, freezing me from the inside out. His eyes are bloodshot; his skin faded and dull. He must have slept like shit. I wonder if it's God or me, or Emily, or both. His eyes hold me in place, and he looks like he might cry. "It's the only choice."

"Only choice?" I raise my voice, stepping toward him. "Robert, of course, you have another choice." I reach for his hand. "You could leave all of this behind. You could be with me and..."

"No!" he snaps, backing away from me. "I can't." Tears fall down his cheeks. I've never seen him cry before, and the sight makes my heart stop in my chest. "You don't understand. Something is wrong with me. Before I came to the seminary, I was broken, so broken that I hurt everyone around me. I'd never known love and would squash any morsel that came my way, using people just for pleasure. I care about you, Laurent, more than I've ever cared about anyone before, but I can't hurt you. I can't curse you to my fate."

I push into him, cupping his jaw. "I'm not weak, Robert. Don't worry about me. I can take whatever you throw at me."

He jerks out of my grasp. "You don't understand. It's not just you. It's her, too."

"What do you mean?"

"These feelings. I know I haven't known her long, but I want her. I had a crazy thought that maybe taking her in that confessional booth would cure everything. I'd get my reprieve and be done with her—just like the other women I'd been with in my past. But that didn't happen. She swallowed my come and looked at me, and I just wanted more. Not just sex, but all of her. It was like the way I've always felt about you. Like she sees me for what I truly am and welcomes me anyway. I can't have you both, and even if I have one of you, I'll hurt the other. It's a slippery slope to my ruin and everyone around me. It's as if the devotion I've had for God is misplaced. I can hurt God, but humans are weak, and I can't bring myself to damn you or her with my wicked mind."

A grin cracks my expression, and I turn away from his eyes. "You're so in your head that you never stop to think about the people around you."

"I know, it's just..."

"No. Stop. Do you honestly think either of us are the jealous type? Do you not understand what's going on here? It's the same for me. All this time, I've been devoted to you—guised under my love for God. You were the only one that made me feel whole, but then Emily came, and she saw me for what I am. She had me in any form, and I wanted her too. The feelings I feared would live and die with you multiplied, and I could see my soul in her eyes. I want the same thing you want. I want both of you—completely. There's nothing wrong with you." I run my hands up his chest, feeling his breath rattle in his lungs.

"No, you say that, but it can't work. It's not right…"

"Oh, shut up." I press forward, capturing his lips with mine. I'm always making the first move, but this is what he needs me for—to stop the ramblings in his head and force him to melt. It's immediate this time. He kisses me back hungrily, his hands tangling in my shirt.

My heart races, and I breathe into his mouth as his tongue shoots out and explores me. This isn't like our last kiss. He's surrendered, and he grabs and nips as if he wants all of me. His hands fall down my abdomen until they're at my belt, undoing my binds. He dives his hand under my pants and briefs, and I hiss once his fingers touch my cock. I moan into his mouth as his hand wraps around my length, pulling away from his lips and resting my forehead against his. I need to brace myself. It's already too much.

He pulls me completely from my pants. I'm so hard—harder than I've ever been. He removes his hand, and I gasp, hoping this isn't the end. He spits in his palm and returns it to my shaft, rubbing me up and down slowly. I want to whisper dirty things and confess my love for him, but I'm afraid to say anything and knock him out of his trance.

He brings his lips back to mine, licking my lips and my tongue as he strokes me gently. I thank the Lord for his haste as I try my best to live in this moment, to soak in the feel of his large and rough hands around my cock, applying the perfect amount of pressure as he strokes up and down, lubricating his hand in the precum at my tip before stroking again.

I'm afraid to move at all—to scare him away, but I need his dick in my hands. I've dreamed of the weight of him, of the feel of his come coating my hand, my mouth, inside of me. I'll take whatever I can get. I gather my nerves, inching my fingers into his waistband, moving as slowly as possible. Finally, I feel his erection, as hard and large as mine. He moans into my mouth, shuddering and interrupting his strokes. I freeze, afraid he'll pull away, but he collects himself and continues fucking my mouth with his tongue and stroking my cock.

He's not running away this time. I can feel it. We're no longer priests. Just men—men who sometimes turn into vegetables, but not now. No, there's nothing to stop us from completely giving in to one another. I dive my hand in and pull him out. "Fuck," he mutters into my lips as I stroke him up and down.

His words sound like music. I continue moving my hand around him, hoping to coax out more than come—his feelings, love, everything inside of him.

"Oh, fuck that's so good." He tilts his head back, and I kiss up his neck, over his Adam's apple. He loses his focus. His pumps become staggering. I don't mind. I'll come just from watching him like this. Helpless to my touch, fragile and limp in my arms, even as his dick pulses in my hand.

I wet my lips. "I want you to come all over me," I whisper into his ear. "I want to mix our seed together until we're one." It's a risk, but he seems to like my words, his breathing heavies. "You look so perfect with my dick in your hand. I bet you'd look even better with it in your mouth or your ass."

"Fuck," he cries. He's so close. He's still stroking me, slowly and with a tight grip. I increase my speed, so close to my edge, and needing him there with me. He cries out in a horse, desperate moan. His semen runs over my hand and down my arm. "Good boy, such a good boy." I follow after him, switching my view from his face melting in pleasure to his cock spurting over my hand. It's the most wonderful sight I've ever seen. I could think of a million more beautiful images like his come over Emily's tits while I take him from behind or him erupting in my mouth as I take his cock, and he eats Emily's pretty cunt. God, even in my absolute bliss, I miss Emily.

The room quiets, and the only sound is our labored breaths. I kiss his temple. It's the wrong thing to do. He pulls away, his eyes finally open, and sear into mine. It's like a deer in headlights. I already know where this is going. "No." I shake my head, my hand gripping his arm. He's stronger and pushes away, tucking himself back into his pants. "Robert, stop. We're done with hiding."

He straightens himself and walks past me. "Robert, I love you," I yell, and he stops at the door. "Don't do this to me. I love you. I will love you no matter what form you take. Man, priest, tomato, even in death, my heart will beat for you, and there's nothing you can do about it."

He clenches his jaw, tears forming in his eyes, but he won't look at me. "You'll move past this. It's for the best." And with that, he's gone.

21
Emily

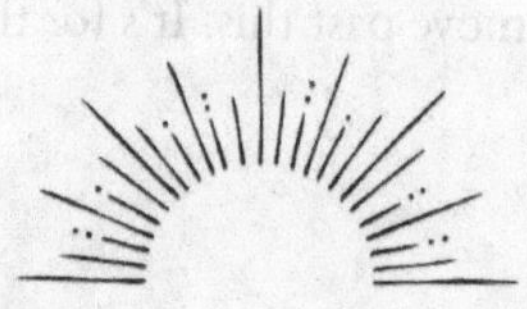

There's something seriously wrong with me. I'm a fucking degenerate. Did I really think I could be in a relationship with two priests who sometimes turn into vegetables? I should be euthanized. Seriously.

I'm alone in the woods on the outskirts of the fields. I can't risk being in the house or out in the open and stumbling on Robert or Laurent. It's too tense, and I don't have the right words yet. I ran into Gail earlier this morning when I was leaving the kitchen. She saw me from the office across the field and shifted her gaze to the ground before speed-walking back inside. Thank God. Facing her is even more terrifying than facing the priests. Or should I say men, because although I haven't talked to them since dinner last night, I'm pretty sure they're not priests anymore, thanks to me.

I have to remind myself not to take all the blame constantly. Sometimes, it seems like self-loathing is a symptom of womanhood. They're the ones married to God—not me, and it's not like I made them fuck me. Well, besides the time I fucked them as vegetables, and they had no say in the matter, but every other time they were very much the instigators. It's not like this sort of thing happens often—the whole tempting men out of their vows. I'd barely tempted a man-eating monster. I don't necessarily scream seduction. Something's different between the three of us. It's like we're all sucked into the same black hole, and there's no chance of escaping—like we're made for each other.

No. That's crazy. I've been reading too many romance novels. They're just hot and horny from not fucking for the last fifteen years. That combination can make anyone feel all magical and predestined for one another. Right?

I sigh, falling back against the forest floor and staring at the canopy of leaves overhead. Birds chirp in the distance, and a breeze blows across my skin. I try to place my mind in the moment, but all I can think about is the last time I was here with Laurent, and he fucked the shit out of me in his rubber ducky sweater—well, previously in his rubber ducky sweater.

A chill runs up my spine at the memory of his face between my legs, ringing out every ounce of pleasure in my body. I would do anything to relive that moment again. I'd do anything to even live in the moment of last night, as fucked up as that sounds. And that's how I know something is wrong with me. A woman was scared mentally, and two men lost their job, and I still just rather be fucking the priests. Hell, I probably lost my job, too, now that I think about it. Oh well. It's not like I'd want to stay here. Sure, it's peaceful and fulfilling, but it would hurt too much to be in this place without them.

What's next for me? I'm about to be homeless, and I need a plan, but it seems that no matter where I go, I'm just going to fuck things up—literally. I can just see it. I get a job as a janitor, and the next thing I know, I'm fucking a mop and a duster. I laugh at my own stupid joke, covering my hands with my mouth. I'm ridiculous.

Maybe the priests had the right idea. Maybe I should become a nun. That way, I'd never be around men who could hurt me. There's got to be a nunnery without any priests. I don't think I could handle being around another priest again unless they are old and unattractive, which is probably how most priests look anyway. So maybe I can be around priests, just not my priests.

That settles it. I'll join a nunnery. A place where I can't ruin other people's lives and can't be hurt by men. It's the perfect set-up. Except, even as my mind comes to this conclusion, I don't feel any better. I don't want to be a nun. I want to be with them, but that's not an option. Not even close.

The idea of running away with Laurent rings like a shiny bell at the corner of my hope. He did suggest the idea before he fucked me over the table, but it can't happen. I could live a good life with Laurent, yes. Filled with laughter, joy, and endless orgasms, but I don't think it would be enough for either of us. Last night was groundbreaking—all three of us engaged in each other's pleasure. Nothing would compare to that moment. It would forever be jaded by what could be. I know Laurent well enough to know it would be the same for him, too.

Men are ruined for me now. Nothing will ever compare to all three of us together. It's a fact. Nunnery, here I come, whether I like it or not.

I sigh and sit up, ready to turn in and iron out the details of my plan, when a twig snaps behind me. I whip around to the source, my heart pounding, but nothing is there. Maybe it's an unseen bird or squirrel. It's the most logical explanation, but my heart still hammers in my chest. I'm being ridiculous. Being murdered in the woods is the least of my worries right now. I turn back around and scream, scrambling backward. An old woman squats before me. She has dark hair streaked with gray. A stained smile graces her face, and her smokey eyes pin me in place. A black cloak drapes her small frame. I could overtake her if she meant me harm, but it doesn't make her presence any less terrifying.

"Do not be afraid, child," she says sweetly.

"What the fuck are you doing?" I yell because she appeared out of nowhere, inches from my face. I don't care if she's telling me not to be afraid—any sane person would be. I move backward on my hands and feet until my head meets a tree trunk.

"I didn't mean to frighten you. I was brought in on the wind."

I catch my bearings enough to get to my feet. "Yeah, whatever, lady. I don't know who you are, but I'm getting the fuck out of here." I don't want to leave my back to her, but I've seen way too many horror movies to know how this ends. I'm not staying and playing her game. I turn away to walk back to the parish.

"I think I can help you with your priests. Or should I say your little produce pals?"

I stop in my tracks. As much as every cell in my being urges me to flee and escape my imminent death, I have to hear her out. This must be the old woman that said that creepy shit to Robert and Laurent the day before they turned into vegetables. She must be the key to all of this.

I turn back to her, and she hobbles up from her knees. "Did you do this to them?" I step closer, crossing my arms over my chest. Her body shakes slightly as she walks closer to me, as if she is mere seconds away from tumbling to the ground. I should feel sorry for her and rush to her side to steady her, but I'm no fool. She's powerful and threw all of our lives into a tizzy. I'm not falling for her helpless act.

I'm inches away from the large boil on her nose. She parts her lips to speak. "I am only a mere messenger for the cosmos. Nature sometimes plays games with us mortals and asks me to relay their message." The sparkling in her eyes indicates she's enjoying this.

"Okay, so what's the message then?"

She reaches up and places her wrinkled hand on my shoulder. "Oh, dear child. Isn't it obvious?"

"Isn't it obvious why two priests are turning into produce and giving off a sexual aura? No, not exactly." My cheeks heat, realizing what I just admitted to this stranger.

She laughs, loud and scratchy. "Thank goodness I'm here. What would you three do without me?"

I grumble, waiting for her to go on.

She sighs and shakes her head, gathering my annoyance. "My dear child. I already told them the answer: *all that is hidden will be brought to light. They need a transformation. It's up to them to define the true fruits of their souls.*"

"Okay, so they turned into vegetables so I could do with them what they've always dreamed of? Why do they only sometimes turn into vegetables, and how do we get it to stop?"

"The sex is only part of their desires. The key is their desire to connect, to be a part of a union with their body and soul. Not like they are with their religion. That is all a front to mask what they truly are."

I wait for more. That didn't answer any of my questions. "Okay?" I say with a bit of an attitude. I need to watch it, or next thing I know, I'll be turned into a pumpkin.

She sighs, her rosy disposition shifting. "You three are destined for each other, cut from the same cloth. The universe wants you three together, and this was how they chose to bring you to each other. They turn into vegetables whenever the three of you are together, and at least one of you admits your desires to yourselves, while the other denies their true feelings."

My mind races with all the instances they turned into vegetables. What about the first time they turned into vegetables? I wasn't there in the field with them? Maybe they didn't turn until I was only a few paces away, like we guessed, or maybe it was just a fluke since it was the first time. It seems pointless to harp on the details. There's so much to still uncover. "So basically, this is Robert's fault?"

"There have been times when each of you pretended this was something less than what it truly was."

"Why didn't I turn into a vegetable then?"

She shrugs. "It wasn't needed of you."

None of this makes sense, but what did I expect? Physics? I've been having sex with vegetables. Nothing is normal or linear about this situation.

She goes on, "Last night, all three of you gave yourself to your urges, unafraid to release your souls from their binds."

My body clamps in horror. "Have you been watching us?" God, this is getting worse and worse.

She laughs. "Oh no. Do not worry. The universe whispers to me the goings of your relationship."

I eye her skeptically. She seems like a freaky little woman. I don't know if I believe her, but I don't have time to hound on the unnecessary details. "So now what? What do we need to do to stop them from turning into vegetables?"

"All three of you must admit your love for each other. Then you can live in your true forms."

Love? I just met these two. How can I admit to loving them?

She smiles at me as if reading my thoughts, which is completely possible. She is a magical being, after all. "Don't think about it too much. Your heart knows the truth."

My mind replays all our moments together—the good and the bad. I close my eyes and remember the way my blood felt, as if it was riddled with magnets only charged to them. I've been jealous of their connection, but maybe all of those intense feelings were something more. Maybe it was love. Maybe it was love designed by the universe. Maybe I fit into their love story in the same poetic way. But reality dawns on me.

"Robert will never admit he loves us. He's in too deep."

The woman sighs. "Yes. That is why I am here. It seems that nature isn't able to take its course with that one."

"So now what? They stay turning into vegetables?"

"No. If you all go your separate ways, then the transformation will never happen again."

My heart sinks. Just what I feared. They don't need me. Selfishly, I wish the curse made it harder for us to part, even if it meant forcing them to their vegetable forms, but that thought only lasts a moment. I want them to be happy most of all. "Great, perfect."

"I think we both know that's not how you feel."

"Well, there's nothing I can do about it."

She gives me a knowing smile, placing her hand on my cheek. "Your destiny isn't over, child. Be patient and bear your feelings boldly."

"But..." I blink, and she's gone.

I swivel my head to the empty forest around me, blinking rapidly to catch her in the corners of the woods. She's gone, but maybe she was never here. Maybe my mind is playing tricks on me. No, it felt too real. As real as the connection between Robert and Laurent. But just like the three of us, it doesn't matter. There's no use fighting to bring her back or to make Robert confess his love to us. It's over. The universe has it wrong.

22

Robert

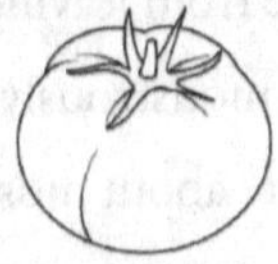

I'm leaving the place I called home for the past fifteen years. I spent the day arranging the details of my new dwelling at the monastery and organizing paperwork for the new priest—whoever he may be. It's shitty that I'm leaving my congregation without an explanation, but I'm too much of a coward to face them. I can't tell a lie, and I can't tell them the real reason I'm leaving—because I was jerking myself off while watching my brother in Christ fuck our cook.

Of course, I could explain how it's so much more than that. Emily isn't just someone to fill our sexual needs, and Laurent isn't just another person in power who will keep a secret. It would seem that way to the outside eye, but they don't understand the draw I have to both of them—the connection I must sever before I seriously hurt someone. It's better to leave without a goodbye—to run away and never look back.

It's late as I pack my few belongings into worn suitcases I haven't pulled out of my closet in years. I'm doing my best to stay quiet, but my mind keeps wandering, making me clumsy and dropping various items. When I drop one of my shoes, I still, listening to hear if I woke anyone. It's silent. My heart pangs. A part of me wants someone to get up—to confront me one last time and stop me from leaving. But no, that would be selfish. I've already been monstrously self-absorbed, dragging down the two people I care about most. I can't let my heart get in the way of what's right again.

My heart breaks for Laurent. A part of me regrets the moment we shared in our office, stroking each other's cocks until we erupted into each other's hands. Another part of me thanks the Lord that I at least have that moment to reflect on for the rest of my lonely days—the selfish part of me, of course. Laurent deserves better. He deserves someone to love him as reverently as he's loved me, for someone to love him and only him. I can't be that person. I've always held room for someone else. At first, it was God. Now, it's Emily. It's unfair, and I know he'll appreciate my decision to leave when he's happy and in love with someone less broken.

Laurent and I have years of connection ripped apart, but Emily is the one I truly mourn for. She didn't deserve any of this. She came to the parish to seek refuge and start a new life. She escaped an abusive relationship and ended up with my toxic ass ruining everything. I took my authority and her vulnerability and contorted her to my whims. I tried my best to fight my urges, but I didn't try hard enough. I could have withstood the temptation if I had been a better man. Even when I turned into a tomato, and she rubbed me against her clit, I should have let that one mishap be the end of everything. I shouldn't have let my mind ping-pong back and forth—trying to use God's will to fit my desires.

"What am I doing?" I ask myself, setting down the shirt in my hand. I can't just leave without explaining things to Emily—without apologizing. I must let her know it's not her; it's me, as cliche as that sounds. She's beautiful, lovely, perfect—all the wonderful things in this world. I'm tainted, damaged, and a beacon for destruction. I can't bring her with me to hell. She deserves so much better, and she needs to know that.

I check the clock on my bedside table. It's two in the morning, but I'll chicken out if I don't go to her now. Before I have a second to think, I leave my bedroom and march toward Emily's room, looking down at my feet the whole way to practice what I'll say. I'm so busy in my head that I don't even realize Laurent's outside her door until I bump into him. I fall backward, landing on my ass.

"What are you doing?" he asks, rubbing where our heads crashed together.

But before I can answer, Emily's door swings open. She looks down at us, as beautiful as ever, in a silk nightgown. Her chocolate brown hair lies over her shoulders, hitting the peaks of her breasts. I blink, and everything grows.

"Oh, my God!" Emily exclaims, now much larger, and looks down at me with a hand over her mouth. I don't even have to try to move to know what has happened. I'm a fucking tomato. What great fucking timing.

She looks down the hall before scurrying to grab us and shut us in her room. "You two are ridiculous," she says quietly as she shuffles on slippered feet over to her bed. If I had a tomato dick right now, it would be rock-hard. Does she really want us so badly that she's not even wasting time contemplating? Just jumping into her bed and getting down to business? God, this girl is perfect.

To my dismay, she places us before her, crossing her arms over her chest and tucking her legs underneath her. "We need to talk," she says. She sighs, looking up at the ceiling. "God, I'm talking to fucking vegetables." She shakes her head. "No, we're past this." She turns her attention back to us and God, is it one of the loveliest privileges to hold her gaze. "I don't know why you both were at my door so late at night, but from the fact that you're both vegetables, I know one of you wasn't coming here, to be honest. I'm looking at you, Robert." She squints at me.

What is she talking about? Was I coming to lie to her? Maybe I'm even lying to myself.

"I don't know what's going to happen tomorrow or the next day or where this crazy life will take us, but I know if I don't tell you both this, then I'll regret it for the rest of my life." She takes a big breath, her eyes watering. She turns away from us. "I love you two." She chokes on her words. "I know, it's crazy, and it doesn't make sense, and who do I think I am that I can be in love with two men at the same time? But it's true. It's weird and complicated and doesn't make sense, but it's real. There's a connection between the three of us—one that surpasses any humanly form. We were made for each other. I can feel it in my bones. I've always wondered what people were talking about when they described faith in God even though they had no proof, but I think this is it. I just know in my heart that I love you two and I don't need a reason, and I don't even need you two to love me back. All I need is to tell you both."

I'm vibrating. Of course, I'm aroused because whenever I'm around Emily or Laurent, I'm aroused, but this is so much more than that. Emily's words unlocked something in me. It's like she spoke the unsaid truth of my heart—the part I shoved away and was too afraid to admit. I love them both, just like she loves us both. It's not crazy or selfish. What we have together is otherworldly. It doesn't live by the rules of society.

It's so clear to me now. I love her. I love Laurent. I urge to scream it from the rooftops, but I can't because I'm a stupid fucking tomato. The shaking increases until I can't see anything in front of me. Everything goes black, but it only lasts a moment. I blink, and I'm seated on Emily's bed. Laurent sits beside me, staring down at his human arms and legs. Emily sits before me, wide-eyed.

"What happened?" she asks. I move forward, grabbing her neck with my human hands and pulling her lips to mine. I kiss her. Electricity zips through me. Her lips on mine are better than any substance—better than God. I could live in this moment for eternity. I desire to drive my tongue into her mouth and taste more of her sweetness, but I pull back. Her eyes flutter open, dazed and confused. "I love you," I say before kissing her again.

She reaches for me, running her hands up my front, unbuttoning my shirt. I want to give in to her touch, take her, and let her take me, but there's something I need to do first. I pull back, turning to Laurent.

His eyes are wide, his hair disheveled. I can nearly feel his heart racing. I remove the distance between us, placing my lips on his. He stills for a moment—shocked, but then snaps out of it, opening for me to enter, kissing me with familiarity and newness. His hands dig into my hair, pulling me closer and closer, but I find the strength to pull back. "And I love you too," I whisper against his lips.

"You do?" The question breaks my heart—his voice so weak around the words.

"I've always loved you, Laurent," I murmur before returning my lips to his. The whole world around us fades. It's just him and me and our bodies morphing into one. Emily's bright light never fades from my consciousness, though. I need her here with us. If only I could have two mouths to devour both of them.

Just when I'm about to pull back to kiss her again, alternating between the two until I've had my fill, she places her hand on my lap. I pull away from Laurent. "No," she says softly. "Don't stop kissing him. It makes me so happy to see you two like this."

My heart nearly floats out of my chest. This is what I've only dreamed of. She wants me to kiss Laurent. Our love for each other is the same and multiplied by three.

I look down as Emily dives into my sleep shorts, pulling out my cock. She pulls out Laurent as well—our shafts standing proudly, just inches from each other. I suck in a breath as Emily brings her lips to the head of me, lathering me with her tongue and taking me in deeply. She removes her lips and switches to Laurent, repeating the same movement with him. Our dicks are lubricated with her saliva, and she strokes us, jerking us off at the same time.

"Kiss each other," she begs. My lips thirst for her—this beautiful, perfect woman, but I also don't want to let this moment pass. I don't know what the morning will bring, but I know I won't be without them. There will be many opportunities to live out every combination between us.

I crash my lips against Laurent, running my fingers through his coarse strands. He moans into my mouth as Emily strokes us slowly. I'm thankful for her tempo. I don't want to lose myself yet. I desire both of them in so many ways, but most importantly, I want us all coming simultaneously.

Laurent pulls away from my lips, and I rest my head against his cheek, doing my best to control myself. He grabs Emily's shoulder, and she stops stroking us, her hands still wrapped around our cocks. "I love you, Emily. I loved you from the first moment I saw you, as crazy as it sounds."

His words make my dick harder. It's odd to love them so much that I'm not jealous when the other confesses their love. It just makes me happier—and hornier.

"Laurent, I love you so much," Emily says through a breathy gasp, continuing to move her hands up and down. It's like her stroking our cocks at the same time is as sensual for her as it is for us.

It's too much, and from Laurent's heavy breathing, he's nearing his edge, too. I don't want to finish like this. I grab Emily's hand, staring deep into her eyes. "I want to watch him fuck you again." At my words, Laurent flings off his sleep shirt and shorts, not letting his eyes leave us while he does so.

Emily nods, crawling onto Laurent's lap but still facing me. He grabs her, kissing down her neck as she lifts her night-gown overhead and throws it to the side. She's not wearing any panties—my perfect little angel, completely bare for us.

I rip my shorts off completely and throw my shirt overhead. I need to be naked and feel every moment of this. I need her taste on my lips. Before she sits down on Laurent's dick, I duck down, running my tongue up her slit. "Oh God," she yells.

I pull back, clamping my eyes to compose myself. "You taste so fucking good." Last time, I was a bystander, this time, I want to be an equal participant in their delight.

She's dripping, ready to take all of Laurent. I watch as she lowers herself onto his glistening dick. She cries out once she meets his hilt, taking all of him like a good little girl.

Laurent throws his head back. "God, she's so good. She takes me so good."

I lower back down, flicking her hardened clit with my tongue. I need her to come multiple times—the first one while she's riding Laurent's dick. Emily rolls her hips, and I try my best to follow her. As much as I want her on my tongue, the position makes it difficult to hit her right. I sit up and kiss her mouth.

She moans into me as my fingers find her heat between her legs. I rub her just the way I know she likes, just like she rubbed me against her when I was a tomato. I start out with longer slow strokes, teasing her once I reach her clit. She bounces faster on Laurent's lap, creating more friction on my hand.

"Oh, fuck," Laurent cries. I don't want him to come yet, so I focus all my attention on her bundle of nerves, flicking her with the perfect amount of pressure. I pull back to watch her face contort as her first orgasm washes over her. "Oh, yes!" she cries, her eyes clench as her body spasms under my touch.

Laurent turns his head to the side, shutting his eyes and biting his lips—clearly holding himself back. It's the most perfect sight I've ever seen. The two of them, sweating, drunk on the ecstasy of each other, but I know it won't compare when we're all coming at the same time.

I grab the back of Emily's neck, pulling her into an abrasive kiss. "I want to fuck you now." The words vibrate on my mouth, just inches from her lips. I reach behind her to Laurent, pulling him into a hungry kiss. "And I want you to fuck me," I whisper against his lips.

There are so many ways I picture myself tangled with Laurent and Emily, but this seems like the perfect start to our cosmic beginning. I'm used to calling the shots. Of course, I want to hear and live out all of Laurent and Emily's desires, but I want them to know, right now, how much I want them—how much I want to fuck and be fucked by them with no turning back.

"Is this heaven?" Laurent says with a smile, rolling his forehead against mine, the air is already heavy from the thick energy in the room.

"Not yet," I whisper back. In one swoop, I grab Emily by the waist, falling over her on her bed. Her hands snake around my neck as our mouths collide and our tongues search each other. I run my fingers down her body, reveling in the feel of her skin under my touch. Feeling her as a human doesn't even compare to the feeling of her skin as a tomato. Now, I can touch her the way I please—the way I know she wants me to worship her. I seek out the heat between her legs, already dripping and sensitive. She moans into my lips as I stroke her. She's so ready for me, and I can barely take the anticipation.

"I don't know how long I'll last." I groan. It's been a long time since I've buried myself in someone. Just the thought makes my tip leak. I've never had someone enter me from behind, and I have a feeling it will be too great, too quickly. Thankfully, we have eternity together—until death and even after that to explore each other's bodies in every which way.

As if reading my mind, Emily replies, "That just means it will be quicker until we can do this again." She runs her hand down my cheek. I stare into her eyes, lost in her beauty—falling down an endless hole if I don't stop myself. I grab my cock and position myself at her entrance. A chill runs up my spine at the thought that I'm entering the place Laurent just filled—that he stretched her cunt just moments before. I crave to be deep inside her with him. She's made to take both of us. But not right now. Now, I need him in me.

I give a sharp and short thrust, crying out once Emily's pussy wraps around me. "You're so tight," I cry in disbelief. Our cocks are practically the same size—large and long, but Emily's cunt feels as if she's never been fucked. It's too good for my weak mind right now.

Her nails dig into my back, and she bucks against me, urging me deeper. I heed her request, pushing myself to my base and not stopping until I hit her wall. She cries out, and I kiss her cheek, wanting this to last forever, even as I feel myself building to no return.

Laurent folds over me, kissing up to my ear and whispering. "You look so good fucking her. I could watch you both forever." His hand runs down my back until he reaches my ass, grabbing my cheeks and giving one a sharp slap. "God, I've dreamed about this, Robert. You have no idea."

I turn my head to reply, "Oh, yes, I do. I was right there in your dream with you."

His finger finds my hole, circling the rim gently. I've never taken anything before, and the thought should scare me. Laurent is large, and although I know it will be glorious to have him inside of me, I know there will be pain, but I welcome it freely.

I don't move inside Emily. I kiss her gently. It's too much, and if I move an inch, I'll come inside of her.

Laurent continues to circle my rim until he inserts his finger inside of me. I clench on instinct, but he doesn't stop, entering softly but firmly. I relax as my body shifts from discomfort to bliss. I moan into Emily's mouth as he increases his speed. He pulls out his finger, spitting, and then fits inside me again—this time with another finger. Again, it's intense pressure at first, but my body relaxes quicker this time. I immediately want more, and I rock my hips back.

"Greedy already." He moans, pulling himself out, spitting, and entering again with three fingers. "Fuck!" I moan, urging everything in me not to explode.

"You're taking me so good, Father. I think you're ready for all of me." I wonder if he'll always call me Father. Oddly, I enjoy it. It reminds me that right now, I'm doing something I've always dreamed of. I'm doing what I was never supposed to do as a priest. It's fucking hot.

He removes himself. "Fuck her while I fuck you," he orders before spitting on my hole. I do as I'm told, thrusting in and out until I feel Laurent's tip press against me. With each of my thrusts, he enters more and more. Thank God he prepared me with his fingers because I'm instantly full—the pressure immense. But Emily's still so tight and feels so good that I can't even notice the pain.

He gives a hard thrust, and then he's completely inside of me. "Laurent!" I yell. He kisses the back of my neck. "That's a good boy, taking all of me." He whispers through his moans.

It takes a few moments, but we finally match our thrusts—fucking into Emily at the same time. I do my best to hold us both back, to not crush her under our weight. With my arms outstretched, I watch as her tits bounce and her expression shifts into a soft and malleable perfection. "So beautiful and perfect," I murmur, barely forming words and mostly desperate sounds.

It's building quickly. I increase my speed, and so does Laurent. I'm filling Emily so completely, hitting the other side of her, that I know she's close to her edge. This is it. The moment the gods have been waiting for. They turned us into vegetables and defied the laws of physics for this moment. And as the warmth fills me and my vision tunnels out, I realize why.

I cry out, atoms exploding through me as I burst into Emily, filling her. Laurent follows right behind me, filling me. It's like our moans morph together into one beautiful symphony. We're sputtering into each other, becoming one flesh. I drown in the ecstasy, unafraid of ever coming out of the delirium. I rest against Emily's chest, still holding our bodies up as Laurent slumps against me. We catch our breaths against each other, and

I listen. I listen to the sweet sound as our hearts beat to one rhythm, to one tune, as if we truly are one.

23

Emily

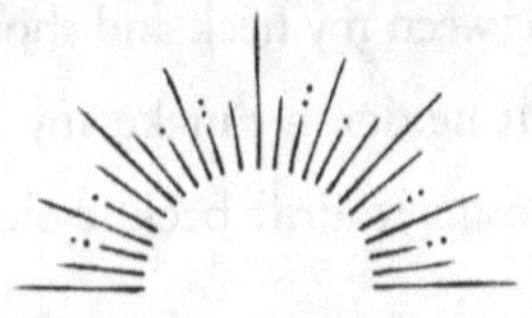

A noise wakes me from my sleep—a constant chirping in the distance. My body's too heavy, though. I can't remember the last time I felt this good. My consciousness slowly washes away the fog of my sleep, and I remember where I am, registering the flesh rubbing against my own. The events of last night swirl around me, and my giddy grin appears. I open my eyes and look over at the two gorgeous men sleeping on either side of me. Not just any men—my men. Men sent by God just for me.

Weeks ago, I felt like the ad for the parish cook job was a message of hope from the heavens. Now, I know how right I was. This job didn't just give me a new start; it gave me my endgame.

I cuddle into the blankets, rubbing against both of them. Laurent wraps an arm around me and pulls me in close. I revel in his touch, but I can't help focusing on Robert's reaction. He confessed his love to me last night—to us. It was plain and simple and left me with no doubts, but he's notorious for changing his mind. This is the last piece to show me he's certain about us.

I exhale once Robert blinks, and a smile warms his face. I smile back. He scoots closer to me, kissing my forehead and tucking his head between my neck and shoulder. His erection presses my side, but he doesn't make any attempt to further our intimacy. He seems to drift back to sleep, soothed by my presence.

That's it. That's all I need. He's in this for real, and this morning is the start of our new life together. There's so much to figure out, but I'm not worried, as long as we're together.

I sit in the comfort of the two for a few more moments, my mind recalling the intricacies of last night, Robert fucking me while Laurent fucked him. I've never felt so full, wanted, and understood. Everything made sense in that moment. We were made for each other and it was clear by how perfectly we all three fit together. I don't have to worry about them turning into vegetables anymore. Even though I can't deny I enjoyed pounding myself with them as produce, this is much, much better.

The kitchen door shuts, and I tense. Robert nor Laurent stir, and they look so peaceful that I don't want to wake them. I sit up, gingerly maneuvering around the two and out of bed. Before I exit my room, I watch them. Robert swings an arm over Laurent, pulling him close. Robert kisses Laurent on his head, and Laurent nestles under his chin. The two fall back into their slumber in each other's arms. I nearly cry at the sight. It's so intimate, so natural. I'm so lucky to witness it—to view them in their true form, finally. They've never looked more beautiful.

I pull a robe around me before slipping out of the room, careful not to make noise when I shut the door. I tread lightly down the hall until I catch Gail making a cup of coffee in the kitchen. The damn creaky wooden floors give me away, and she turns to me once I step into view.

"Good morning," she says, bringing a mug to her lips and taking a sip.

"Good morning," I reply, my cheeks immediately heating. I hoped the three of us could run away without having to deal with anything, but that was wishful thinking. Gail had been kind to me and offered me the job. The least I can do is apologize for fucking out in the open where she could walk in and tell her I'm quitting. Actually, I probably don't need to tell her that. I'm pretty sure I'm fired.

I walk to the kitchen island, pull out a bar stool, and sit, keeping my eyes down. I've never been good with confrontation, and this situation is more awkward than most. I gather my words, but before I can say anything, she places a white mug in front of me. I pick up my gaze, catching her eyes as she stares over the counter at me, leaning as if she's planning to stay awhile.

"Thank you." I smile shyly and take a sip. I place it back down on the counter and sigh. "Gail, I'm so sorry you walked in on that. We thought you would be gone for a few more days, and there's a bunch of other stuff happening that's too crazy to explain." I can't bring up the whole vegetable situation. This woman will commit me to a mental hospital or run me off the property with a torch.

She scoffs, looking down at the counter and shaking her head. I prepare for a tongue-lashing. "I can't say I'm surprised to walk in on those boys with one another, but seeing you thrown in the mix did catch me off guard."

"What?"

She laughs, and her eyes meet mine. "Please, it was obvious they were keen for each other. I'm a good Catholic woman, but I will always root for true love."

Of course. Anyone could see they were in love, and Gail had been around for much longer than I had. She must think I'm a slut for coming in between them. How do I explain we're all in love with each other?

"Well, you don't have to worry about us being inappropriate anymore. We'll be leaving."

Her eyes widen. "Together? As in all three of you?"

My face burns brighter. "Yes. We're going to be together. We love each other."

"Huh, love, you say?" She turns to the side as if thinking my sentiment over. I can't expect much from her. If someone told me that they were about to run off to be in a polygamous relationship, I'd roll my eyes and cringe, but my brain has been rewired, along with my organs being rearranged. I'm basically a new person now.

She sighs. "I get it."

This is the most shocking thing she could say. "You do?"

"From what I saw, it was pretty hot. If I were you, I'd be in love, too."

I sputter into a laugh, coffee dripping out of my mouth. She laughs along with me and passes me a napkin to clean up. I regain my breath and shake my head. "Goddammit, Gail, you're surprising me."

She shrugs. "Maybe after all my years on this earth, I see things a little differently."

"Hm, I didn't really peg Catholics for their open-minded-ness."

She shoots me a look. "Really? The two priests you're fucking seem pretty open-minded."

"Touché." I suppress my smile.

"I don't know," she goes on. "I've witnessed so much life that everything seems even more confusing. The more I see, the less I know. I liked religion growing up because it gave me answers, but it no longer seems that way. Maybe I like religion just for the familiarity, to feel like I belong. I think that would be enough for me, just following the motions. I just don't think it's enough to judge or condemn others for living their truth instead of believing other people's wishful thinking."

I sit with her words for a moment. I came to this place to start again, find my purpose. Maybe that's why most people come to God, or religion, or a higher power in general. But maybe there isn't one answer. Maybe everyone has their own truth they have to follow.

"Any idea where you three will go?" she asks, snapping me back as she peers at me over her coffee cup.

I shake my head. "Nope. We'll figure it out, though."

"I heard there's a vegetable farm for sale a few towns away. I suggest somewhere quiet and desolate. The next time someone walks in on you three fucking, they might die of a heart attack. Sounds messy."

I laugh, shaking my head. She's right, though. Quiet sounds nice. If my healthy imagination has anything to do with our future, we'll definitely need some privacy.

24

Laurent

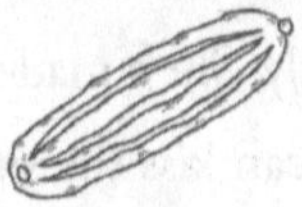

"**A**lmost there, baby. You're doing so good," I whisper in her ear. She cries out, sweat dripping down her temple. We've planned for this. Making sure she was ready for this moment, but nothing could prepare me for how glorious it would be, on the brink of something brand new.

I insert another finger, Robert's dick sliding underneath. He's hard and slick, moving in and out slowly as I stretch Emily. "You're so perfect," Robert murmurs underneath her, kissing her cheek.

She's ready for me. I pull my fingers out, position my cock at her entrance. I push in slowly, nearly finishing from Robert's dick rubbing against mine. "Jesus Christ!" I turn my head to the side, unable to look at Emily's perfect cunt from behind as it takes Robert and I at the same time. I thrust in more, and

Robert and Emily moan in unison. I'm only halfway in, and we're all going to finish before I'm at my hilt.

I thrust in hard, bouncing on Emily's ass, my skin slapping against her. I fold over her, finding an easy tempo, resting my head next to Robert's and Emily's as they kiss. He pulls away from her and brings his lips to mine. "You feel so good against my cock," he mingles between his kisses.

"She fits us so perfectly. She's made for us both," I whisper back, pulling away so I can kiss the side of Emily's face as she moans, lost in the ecstasy of being completely full. It's a sentiment we love to say—that we're destined for each other. We love to remind ourselves of it whenever we feel like things are too good to be true. The witch, angel, or whatever that creepy woman was, said that the gods threw us together. Ever since we confessed our love for each other and broke our vegetable curse, it's been obvious. Who knew three people could be so completely happy together?

It's only been five months since we left the parish and bought the farm, but damn, has it been good, and I know with every ounce of my being, it will last. But this, fucking Emily with Robert's cock sliding against my own—now this takes the cake of everything we've experienced together, and that says a lot.

"I'm so close!" Emily yells, her body tightening underneath me. Her words bring me closer to that edge, and then I feel Robert's cock sputter from underneath mine, and I'm gone—lost in another universe. Our spurts synchronize, and I feel our liquids mixing together and overfilling out of Emily. Is it weird that I want to drink it? All three of our juices mixed together like a delicious come-cocktail? Probably. But Emily did shove my entire body up her vagina when I was a cucumber. I'm pretty sure nothing is off the table for us. We've already discovered our love for role-play. I've dressed up as a cowboy, a pirate, and my fuzzy rubber ducky sweater has even made some special appearances. We love to fuck around, but maybe I'll save the come-guzzling for next time. One new sex-venture a day just to make sure we pace ourselves.

The fog clears, and the world comes back to view. I don't want to move off these two, but I am on the top of our human dog pile. It's only fair to roll off and offer them their freedom. Emily's spent, her eyes still closed and catching her breath. Robert peppers kisses over her face, telling her how good she was. I lean over and join the party—kissing rapidly until her face morphs into a smile. "Okay, okay. You two are going to kiss me to death."

"Oh, I'm sorry." I press my lips against Robert, continuing my pepper of kisses on his lips. Emily laughs, rolling off Robert and onto the other side of him, rubbing at her eyes and stretching.

I move closer to him, running my fingers over his chest as our kiss deepens. "I loved that," I say.

"It was fucking perfect," he replies.

"And the bed held up nicely." I grab the banister behind me and shake it to prove my point. Since moving out here, Robert has been deep in his woodworking, building all the furniture for the house. He just finished our new California King bed, and this was our first test of its sturdiness. As much as I loved cuddling up with the two every night, it will be nice to have a little more room when we *actually* need to sleep.

"I have plenty of more projects in mind, including furniture that has many different uses." He runs his hand through my hair, staring at my lips, his eyes dark and mischievous.

"Oh, yeah. Do you have plans to construct and tie me to a cross, Father?"

"Oh, I'd love to see you tied up." And just like that, I'm rock hard again. I trail my hand down to his cock to find he's hard as well. It's great to know that we don't just get unnaturally horny whenever we're vegetables. Although feeding, bathing, and working have been hard to fit in between our constant fucking.

I'm ready to go for round two, but then I remember our perfect little angel who just graciously took both of our cocks and needs some aftercare. I push back and signal to Emily with my eyes. Robert nods and rolls over, kissing Emily's cheek. I hop over them and lie on her other side, copying Robert. "You're so perfect. I love your face. I love your arm. I love your tits." I kiss over the parts mentioned. My face hovers over her abdomen. "But most of all, I love your... belly button. God, I love your belly button." I kiss the indent in her stomach, swirling my tongue in a little. She laughs but pushes me away. "You are a freak!"

"Yeah, he is a little freaky." Robert pats my cheek. "But that's why we love him."

Emily rubs our arms with a sleepy grin. "Alright, you two. We have a full day ahead of us."

"What?"

"No!"

"You both are the ones that wanted to open a cucumber and tomato farm." She sits up, staring at the puddle of our come below her before jumping out of bed and charging toward the bathroom. She stands in the doorway, the light behind her illuminating her perfect frame. "You can't expect the produce to get up and farm themselves." She slaps her knee, laughing.

"Yeah, no. I've witnessed enough sentient vegetables for one lifetime."

I cuddle in next to him. "Really? I thought you looked rather sexy as a tomato. I wouldn't mind seeing you as one again."

He holds a finger up to my lip. "Don't say that. You will summon the gods to play another trick on us." Since that night in Emily's bedroom at the parish, we haven't turned into vegetables again. The old woman hasn't shown up, and other than our supernatural orgasms, everything has seemed normal. Well, as normal as it can be for a throuple consisting of two ex-priests and a smoking hot chef, living on a rural farm in the middle of nowhere. It's a simple life, filling a hole in me that I yearned to stuff my whole life—literally. Who knew I didn't need religion but that the gods would find me and bring me to my heaven? I wish I knew who to praise. I don't think it's the Catholic God. All of this doesn't really feel like his style.

I guess that's why I thought spending the rest of our lives in nature would be a good idea—honoring whoever chose to bless us with such a bountiful life.

Robert jumps up from the bed, charging after Emily, who squeals in delight. I smile as they kiss, and he backs her into the shower, turning it on without breaking their embrace. Emily screams once the water hits her back but smiles against Robert's lips.

I prop my head up with my arms behind me, watching them. This is my heaven. I need nothing more. I commit this moment to memory, storing it away with all the other beautiful moments we've made together in such a short time.

"Stop watching and get in here, you freak," Robert calls to me, his eyes dark and wanting, beckoning me to him like he's done ever since I've known him. Except now I get to have him. I can touch him, kiss him, fuck him as much as I please, and he'll never turn me away. It's everything I could have ever wanted. Our love story is a weird fucking tale, but it's my favorite. The tale of the veggies who found love.

Thanks for Reading!

Thank you for reading! If you liked *Pounded by Produce: A Veggie Love Tale*, please make sure to leave a review on Amazon and Goodreads. **Want a bonus chapter of one of Laurent and Robert's steamy seminary nights? Subscribe to G.M.'s Patreon.**

Want more of G.M. Fairy? Check out her other books...

Scream for Me: A Dark Monster Love Story

The harbinger of fear, the predator of the night...

I feast on human terror, drinking in their screams like the sweetest nectar. But when I stumble through the portal into her room and hear her cries of pleasure, a far darker, primal hunger takes hold.

She belongs to me now. I need to hear her scream like that again, and I will, even if I have to break her apart.

The woman stolen from her world and thrust into a realm of nightmares...

I felt it—eyes watching me from the darkness, golden and unblinking from the shadows of my closet. The thought sent a shiver through me, twisting into something illicit as I let my fingers wander. But when he pounced, dragging me into his cold, merciless world, the thrill turned to terror.

Now, he demands my pleasure, my screams, but I refuse to surrender without a fight.

Romanced by the Rat: A Ghostlight Falls Story
This rat pulls hair and heartstrings.

When a military science experiment goes wrong, Ramsey wakes up in the body of a rat. He takes refuge in the kitchen of Ratcliffs, a high-end restaurant in Ghostlight Falls. Scavenging for food and dodging danger, he resigns himself to life in the shadows—until she walks through the door.

Charlotte is new in town and looking for a fresh start. Ratcliffs, with its cozy atmosphere and perfect ratatouille, quickly becomes her favorite escape. She doesn't expect to catch the attention of the charming waiter, or for her presence to stir something unexpected in a certain furry onlooker.

Jeremy never wanted to be a server, but the job funds his bodybuilding dreams. When a rat unexpectedly takes the reins, Jeremy finds himself grateful for the unusual partnership. With Ramsey guiding his hands, Jeremy sees an opportunity not just to survive the chaos of the kitchen, but to please the woman of his dreams.

As tension simmers and emotions boil over, the three must decide if they're willing to share this unconventional romance, or if jealousy will ruin the perfect recipe.

The Crimson Wolf: A Red Riding Hood Love Story

Unearthing secrets, unraveling desires, and confronting the primal truth of the werewolf within the woods.

Red, a New York City journalist, returns to her quaint hometown to investigate a string of chilling animal attacks. Determined to unearth the truth, she reconnects with Jack, her childhood first love. The woods hold more than just memories, and a near-fatal encounter introduces her to Cameron, the infuriating and strikingly attractive park ranger with secrets as vast as the forest itself.

As Red delves deeper into the story, she unravels her family's cryptic past and finds herself entwined in a passionate and monstrous conundrum.

With her destiny in her own hands, Red must sift through her heart's tangled desires and the obscured truths of her lineage to discover the real beast of the forest.

Stay up to date on all things G.M. Fairy!